FATAL LIGHT

Also by Richard Currey

Fiction

Crossing Over: A Vietnam Journey

Fatal Light

The Wars of Heaven

Lost Highway

Nonfiction

Medicine for Sale

RICHARD CURREY

FATAL LIGHT

SANTA FE WRITERS PROJECT

Santa Fe Writers Project, SFWP and colophon are trademarks.

Library of Congress Cataloging-in-Publication Data

Currey, Richard, 1949-
Fatal Light/by Richard Currey. —20th anniversary ed.
p. cm.

ISBN-13: 978-0-9776799-2-8
ISBN: 0-9776799-2-6
1. Vietnam War, 1961-1975—Fiction.   I. Title.
PS3553.V6665F38 2009
813'.54—dc22

2008056003

Cover design by Bill Douglas at The Bang
Printed and bound in Canada

Visit SFWP's website: www.sfwp.com and literary journal: www.sfwp.org

Contents

Introduction

A few years ago I visited Cannon Air Force Base. Situated out in the great wide open of southern New Mexico, Cannon is the home of the 27th Special Operations Wing. The occasion of my visit was a National Endowment for the Arts program called Operation Homecoming. In partnership with the Department of Defense and Boeing Aircraft, Operation Homecoming dispatched more than 20 poets, novelists, and journalists to bring writing workshops to veterans of Iraq and Afghanistan at numerous duty stations both within the US and abroad, including in the combat theatre in the Middle East. Operation Homecoming introduced many of our troops to the idea that writing about their military and combat experiences might serve them, the nation, and the greater good in a number of ways. Aside from the possibility that some form of emotional catharsis and at least a step toward psychological healing might stem from self-expression, Operation Homecoming also sought to allay fears that many might have regarding the act of putting words on paper, to explore the mechanics and challenges of the writing process, and looked to foster a safe and tempered environment for all kinds of writers with all manner of notions about how to say what they wanted to say.

I rented a car in Albuquerque and drove the 200 miles southeast to arrive at Cannon's main gate after dark. It was the first time I had been on a military installation in more than 30 years. The gate sentries were officious and vaguely threatening—as they were supposed to be—and asked me to pull into a space adjacent to the guardhouse and wait in the car. I parked and sat and in a moment the base's executive officer arrived. He was a colonel, geared out in field jacket and camos and garrison cap. He smiled and shook my hand and welcomed me on behalf of his commanding officer and said that I was to follow his driver to the BOQ (Bachelor Officers Quarters) where I was "billeted" for the night. The requisite introductory speech concluded, the colonel leaned a bit closer and said that when he learned I was coming he looked up my work, and got hold of a copy of *Fatal Light*.

He told me that he was not a reader, and was generally intolerant of "stuff that's made up." He noted that most of his reading kept to official documents and aviation manuals and an occasional newsmagazine. *Fatal Light* was the first fiction he had read in many years. He thanked me for "keeping the book short," and said he thought the story I told was powerful and surmised that it would ring true to the experience of many. But then he lowered his voice and said, "And it was written by a very angry young man."

My Operation Homecoming colleagues were arriving by then, and the personal moment with the colonel passed. Later that evening, after drinks and dinner and conversation were had and I was back in my room, I stepped out and sat on a wooden bench in a small grassy area. The New Mexico sky was domed and improbably vast, belted with stars. The night hovered, quiet beyond measure except for the sound of the wind, blowing out in the endless blue dark of the desert, and I thought about the colonel's remark. He was a man who, by his own admission, brought no particular sophistication in the ways of novels and storytelling to his reading. He took *Fatal Light* straight on, read without pretension or expectation, and immediately understood the emotional core of the novel— a young combat veteran's sad, dispirited, convoluted, muted rage. The colonel had brought a finger down on the precise heart of the story.

Fatal Light was written in my late 20s and was the evolution of a decade of writing poetry, then prose poetry, and, beginning in 1980, short stories. Most of my working tenets as a writer developed through the disciplines of these short forms. As I evolved toward ever-longer stories (and realized I was becoming a novelist), I wanted to bring the brevity and clarity of focus of the shorter forms I had worked with to a broader storytelling purpose. *Fatal Light* was the culmination of that, and I framed my story with the classic elements of all war stories told over the last 2,000 years: A young man lifted from an innocent life, plunged into the fear and rabid confusion of war, and then, surviving it, left to pick up his own pieces on the long way home. But aside from reflecting my own historical moment and my generation's place in that moment, I wanted to tell an old story from what I hoped might be a different approach, a stripped-down journey through a soldier's life and mind where the nature of war is recalibrated in its purest terms.

Fatal Light drew from some of my own experiences as a Navy corpsman serving with several Marine Corps combat and combat-ready units between 1968 and 1972. But the book is informed not by the literal particularities of my own experience (indeed, most of *Fatal Light* is highly fictionalized), but by the emotional residue of a few years deep inside Marine infantry units, the "grunts" who function as the first phalanx, down where one can smell the earth and the rain and the riven sweat of the men standing behind and in front and on either side. I was an enlisted man serving with mostly other enlisted men in units that were often ordered into action with the barest of rationale, explanation, or any sense that logic or intelligence was at work anywhere in the process. For me, wartime military service was a quintessential existential experience. And, afterwards, there was, at least for me, a well of anger fueled by a sense of purposeless death and cynical manipulation of men and armies for the sake of what I believed to be short-sighted and self-serving political aims.

Years have passed and the fervor of my politicization at the age of 20 has been chiseled by any number of realizations along the way, but I still believe that my old anger was neither misplaced nor inappropriate. Yes, wars are vastly complex affairs poorly served by any attempt to simplify or universalize them. But, still, historical analysis does not and will never blunt the reality that it is the warriors themselves who go home (if they make it home) with the burden. And they become the carriers of war's legacy, experienced by all of them differently but, finally, held in common. And their stories, be they written as the high art of poetry and novels and personal nonfiction, or told over dinner years later at a family gathering, or perhaps never told at all beyond hints and evasions, become an essential part of a nation's fabric, part of that strange post-war blend of pride and regret, honor and sorrow, shame and satisfaction.

Fatal Light is a novel sheared down to the primary essentials of the story it tells and the spiritual predicament it describes, one that has no resolution, no solution, that joins the texture of a life and, as the unnamed young narrator of *Fatal Light* says at one point, sticks there "like a photograph on the spine."

At another point that narrator notes that "war stories are our oldest stories." So it seems, as we now find ourselves slogging through our latest war, two of them, in fact, fought on two fronts. This two-front war's books and poems and memoirs and potent reports from the morphing lines of battle have been arriving. It is another hard dawn for another battered army, and some of its troopers again feel and write and try to come to terms somewhere in their souls and lives. It is a pleasure to see my own contribution to this tradition revived in this beautiful new edition of *Fatal Light*. I hope my view of a kind of universal experience might continue to speak to and resonate with the "Iraq and Afghanistan Generation"—by which I mean not only those of you who have or are now serving in uniform, but all of you. Like the Vietnam Generation before you, your war will mark you, and change you, and, finally, define you.

Richard Currey
February 2009

FATAL
LIGHT

At night in the war I listened to monkeys in the jungle all around me. Low murmur of voices, the clucks and warbles and sighs of monkeys at peace with starlight, and I could rest with their voices knowing that as long as I could hear them I was safe in a ring of darkness, lying there thinking When this is all over and I am out and gone everybody will want to hear the story.

And the story begins like this: There was a boy standing in the middle of America. He was standing in a winter garden with his toy gun strapped on slightly askew, an easy smile, blond hair cut close to the pale skull, rolled-up cuffs on his jeans. The stretch of distance behind him was indistinct, unreal, as if field and horizon had raced on ahead as he stood to turn and look back.

He was a boy who rode his bicycle on early summer mornings, past the elementary school named for Mark Twain and the junior high school named for General Patton, out into the wide boulevard with Ormin's Market at the corner and Henry Ormin sweeping the sidewalk in front of his store window filled with mops and stacks of fruit crates and racks of dusty hats and gardening gloves. The boy had never seen anybody buy a hat or a pair of gloves from Henry Ormin, but hats and gloves lived on in the window, next to the seed envelopes faded by too many sunlit mornings.

The boy's bicycle tires hummed the asphalt and birds foraged on lawns, spooked at his approach: Sudden flutter and crowded whisper of wings, flocks wheeling overhead.

He rode on toward the bridge, riding for the simple pleasure of the open speed, sweat beginning at his hairline and a hard pain above his knees as he pumped against the drag of one gear and balloon tires and an incline, and he slowed on the bridge, halfway across.

I remember: It was only a short bridge over a creek bed but the gorge seemed formidable, falling away to a thin run in the rocks below. I would take my bicycle to that bridge on early summer mornings and stand at the rail feeling the sun was alive and I was steering the sky into luminous places, happy to be the pilot of the tallest air I could find.

MORTAL PLACES

1

My grandfather kept an album. Photographs, newspaper clippings, yellowed squares pasted on black rag pages. An occasional letter folded into the spine. Stained black-and-whites with notes penned in the margins or on the backs: *Uncle Bob Tulley, 1936. With Vallie in California, April 1948.* There were obituaries of family and neighbors, sons dead in the Battle of the Bulge, on Guadalcanal; an account of a cousin's conviction on charges of conspiracy and extortion in the thirties. My grandfather sat beside me as we paged through the heavy book, and he pointed out people, telling their stories. The old photographs seemed always to conceal—shadow days, winter faces—sturdy women watching children or looking away, girls in cottony taffeta, men staring hard and blasted, big-nosed, and tobacco-stained in antiquated suits or huge farmer's overalls; every picture an event: a wedding, a Christmas, a harvest. A cluster in black gathered at the gates of a cemetery. *Bill and Eddie Luke after corn was in. Emma and Tad with kids, Thanksgiving 1943.* My grandfather told me that Tad wasn't in the service in those days because of a clubfoot; he was killed anyway in a thresher accident on the farm, left Emma to go to alcohol and finally suicide, the kids spread out to bitter relatives and orphanages, lost to one kind of destitution or another. There was a picture in the album of me on my second birthday, fat-legged blond on a short ledge with a layer cake, the already extinguished candles leaning into the icing and my face betraying an irritation, a passing anger lost there on that mid-October day. Beyond my grandfather's house, behind me in the picture, massive trees ranged along the Ohio River's eastern shore and through the trees the river itself, vast at that point with glisten and scud and the small frame houses on the opposite shore only squares of white or silver flash in the afternoon sun.

2

In the long summer visits at my grandfather's house I walked the abandoned campsites along the river, under the face of the floodwall that followed the railroad tracks. I pushed sticks through the ashes of spent hobo fires, broke wine bottles against the rails and watched the shards glitter on the roadbed. I stood on the bridge that spanned the river between West Virginia and Ohio, watched freight trains troll by beneath me, hollow roar and tilt, car after car clocking past, desires run distant by time and the force of the land. The trains made a music below the bridge, like my mother always said when she read children's books to me, a long rumble and boom. I walked up the bridge to the imaginary border in the middle of the air where a plaque announced I was about to step into the State of Ohio. There was a low dirty skyline beyond me, factory haze and exhaust smudge. An island drifted downstream, a paradise appearing out of clouds, and a coal barge came toward me, humming a slow wake north.

3

Hand-painted banners announcing the Apple Blossom Festival hung between telephone poles along Main Street. A printer had donated handbills that were nailed to fences and taped inside store windows all over town: a parade, animal rides, bake-off, quilting bee, pie-eating contest. In the afternoon at Dedweiler's pasture there would be aerial barnstormers and at night in the city park the carnival that came every year and a dance in the pavilion with music from the fire hall bluegrass quintet. In that autumn when I turned eleven years old a professional touring group was coming as well, a family of Nashville singers, television smiles and electric guitars and snakeskin western boots, coming to sing on the stage built on festival day by volunteer carpenters from throughout the county.

On the day of the festival traffic into town was already slow by ten o'clock in the morning. Children crossed the streets and the high school marching band drifted toward its collection point on the courthouse lawn, brass and silver shine of trumpets and tubas scattered on ground cloths, uniforms modeled after those of Hessian soldiers in the Revolutionary War: blousy trousers, epaulets and metal buttons and front panels on vests embellished with mothers' and grandmothers' stitchery, a walking fleet of Wellington boots hand-colored white with indigo tassels. I moved beside my grandfather, across the street behind a stalled car and hearing the idle dissonant honks of high school musicians, echo and rattle of snare drums, vendors shouting and somewhere in the distance an automobile horn stuck and moaning. I asked my grandfather for a bag of popcorn from a red cart, and we stopped and my grandfather and the vendor exchanged pleasantries.

Beautiful day for the festival, Bob, my grandfather said.

Yes sir, that it is.

My grandfather told the vendor he should do good business on such a fine day and the vendor said he certainly hoped so and the warm paper sack came down to me aromatic with oil and salt. We walked on with the crowd growing around us, my grandfather at my left shoulder as we edged through shifting groups for a place on the parade route. There was excitement riding out of the sky's span of clean light, and we found a place behind a boy sitting on the curb. I stood between the boy and my grandfather's legs, eating popcorn, watching the north end of Main Street, a long incline to where the high school band would appear.

We could hear the music before we saw the band, drift of the march coming toward us across the air, at first like an afterthought, and the drum major's tall hat rose over the Main Street ridge and behind him, shimmering, levitating into view, the majorettes strutting and kicking. The sparkle of the instruments wobbled up, the drum major turned and blew his whistle and marked time, the fat majorette dropped her baton.

The parade went on forever: Middle-aged men in fezzes riding motor scooters in figure-eights, sad clowns with gigantic red feet and smiling cars that tipped suddenly to their back wheels to turn frantic circles in the street. Sprays of hard candies thrown from floats, the mayor and his polished family in the backseat of a Chrysler Imperial convertible. The Nashville singers on a flatbed truck, stair-step children dressed like Roy Rogers and Dale Evans, sequined silk cowboy shirts with scallops of piping, ranges of fringe and tight pants tucked into boots tooled with intertwined lariats. Waving to the crowd, the eldest son wearing a sombrero, the youngest daughter doing curtseys.

The festival queen and her court rode into view on a float garlanded with tissue flowers, gliding across the horizon of Main Street like a mirage, small-town madonnas sliding past waving their downy arms dreamily, their eyes the eyes of soft animals turned heavenward from thrones of blossoms and crepe, their faces all a magnificent promise, the romance at the end of the world passing so slowly in those long moments of perfect quiet, like the air over the river, the light and stillness inside the world at daybreak, like a held breath.

After the parade my grandfather led me through the crowd, down the hill and west to Juliana Street and Whitlow's Bar and Grill.

Inside the dark bar I climbed onto a stool, everywhere mahogany and sepia and the soft glitter of glassware arrayed under the mirror in front of us. My grandfather pushed his hat back on his head but left it on, a Panama with a black band, and I watched his face in the mirror as he ordered a beer for himself and Coca-Cola for me, talking baseball with the bartender. At the end of the bar a blind man tilted his face to the ceiling, half-finished beer in front of him. The far side of the blind man's body was lit by sunlight from the back door that stood open, his sleeves rolled to where I could see purple tattoos losing their clarity on both forearms. *Well, he ain't the slugger you were in your prime* the bartender was saying as our drinks came with glasses turned upside down over the bottle necks, mine the same as my grandfather's. I poured my Coca-Cola and watched the foam rise; the bartender leaned on the bar in front of us as my grandfather spoke quietly and poured his beer. Traffic sounds filtered from an imaginary distance, time passing in the artificial twilight with no other customers coming in and the bartender and my grandfather talking, now about politics, about Eisenhower. I was finally introduced and the bartender asked my age and how I was liking my visit and by then our drinks were finished. I jumped down from the bar stool to follow my grandfather, and looked back to see the blind man was already gone. An empty beer bottle and an empty glass stood together at the end of the bar. My grandfather touched my shoulder and we were outside, walking toward the bridge and its sudden arch into the sun, disappearing into points west.

4

Mary Meade always said we fell in love in front of Bippo's Pizzeria in Ocean City, Maryland. I had known her for years—elementary school, junior high school—she was the first cousin of Ricky Bayner, who I played football with until he graduated a year ahead of me and went to Yale. I was with Ricky at Bippo's as she wandered the boardwalk with her girlfriends. *Hey,* Ricky had said, *you remember my cousin Mary don't you? Yeah,* I said, *sure, we're neighbors after all.* Ricky and I bought pizza for the girls and we clustered in the back of Bippo's, laughing and playing pinball, and spent that weekend together on the beach, cruising the carnival attractions, Tilt-A-Whirl, The Zodiac, The Scrambler, nervous glances at obscene novelties in the tourist shops, swimming through long afternoons. We rented a surplus navy life raft; Ricky and I inflated it with a bicycle pump and pushed it beyond the breakers while the girls swam out behind us. We drifted the far side of the surf, zinc oxide smeared on our noses, drinking sun-warmed beer and watching the opulent Chesapeake schooners slice past with names like *String of Pearls, Rhonda's Dream, Body and Soul,* in flight toward paradise.

That night we sat on a bench in front of the Mermaid Bar, talking, listening to the ring of arcades and carnival screams and the ocean booming in the darkness behind us, and after the others drifted away Mary and I stayed on, still talking as the neon signs along the boardwalk clicked off and the moon rose higher and we could see a rim of surf break and disappear back into shadow. We slipped off the bench to sit on the sand and kissed, hard and carefully at first, then softer and with more assurance, lying down on the sand and holding each other, watching the moon move from behind the boardwalk façade to flood the beach in a sweep of cold light.

5

In 1967 I was eighteen years old. It was my senior year in high school. Ricky Bayner's older brother was in the army, serving in Vietnam. I had finished my high school football career with six touchdowns in ten games and just under a thousand yards rushing. There was talk of a scholarship to one of the smaller universities. The college scouts believed my speed and agility and fine hands made up for my lack of weight and height, and during that football season the Director of the Selective Service Administration announced that the draft would be intensified due to increased troop demands in southeast Asia.

My grandfather sent me $100 for my birthday, and for Christmas I bought Mary a ring with a diamond inset. On December 28 I received the letter notifying me that my draft classification would revert to 1-A as of graduation day. The letter went on to say that the time and location of my induction physical would be forwarded at a later date.

6

New Year's Eve, 1967. A dark heaven of rock and roll, fall of color, and lives played out in cars. In my Camaro with three other football players, driving, talking, passing around a wine bottle, cruising down the hours and near midnight finding ourselves at the reservoir where we swam and drank and brought girls all through the summer. We got out of the car, crunching leaves, moving like strangers on the landscape. The gravel beach and pier and black water seemed bruised and solitary, no place we had ever been, and the sky was wet with cold moonlight and ragged clouds. Somebody said it was 1968.

The half gallon of cheap sour wine made the round and nobody spoke. After a moment I walked back to my car and sat alone behind the wheel, frightened by a deep and uncertain longing in that expanse of silence.

The news on New Year's Day said Nguyen Duy Trinh, speaking from Hanoi, claimed his government would begin negotiations if the United States would unconditionally halt the bombing of North Vietnam. The New Year's cease-fire was allegedly violated by 170 enemy-initiated actions. There had been fighting at Tay Ninh, 60 miles northwest of Saigon, close by the Cambodian border: 23 Americans were dead, 155 wounded.

By the end of the day Texas A&M had upset Alabama, 20 to 16, in the Cotton Bowl. USC had no trouble with Indiana in the Rose, and I watched Oklahoma squeeze past Tennessee in the Orange Bowl, 26-24. When I turned the television off I felt claustrophobic, vaguely ill. I had received the official letter directing me to report for induction into the armed forces the following November, and I stepped out into cold dusk, shivering. The blue air and hard starlight smelled like smoke. I looked at my car in the driveway, and went inside for jacket and keys.

I drove, through the serenity of quiet winter streets, the already beaten fragility of early demise. Police reports and body counts lived in the radio with psychedelic rock and Detroit soul, a running backdrop. Cultured BBC voices lectured over the shout of gunfire on satellite links from Saigon or Phnom Pen as I drifted the neighborhood lanes and, closer to the city, passed the dark shops and stores in front of their vacant parking lots. I turned the radio off as I moved onto an empty boulevard, and snow began to fall.

7

The night before I left for recruit training I sat in my parents' dining room. My sisters made faces at each other and my father told stories about his years in the service, in the navy during the Second World War and again in Korea.

"There were tough times, sure," he said, sitting back at the end of the meal. "But all in all it was OK. A kid'll pick up things. See things you'd never see anywhere else."

I nodded. My mother looked at her plate and her cheeks were flushed. My younger sister loudly asked to be excused; both girls left the table.

"I'll tell you, though," my father went on. "There was something more—I don't know, organized about World War Two. You went because you wanted to, it was the right thing to do, you were proud to wear the uniform."

"I guess the lines were a little bit more clearly drawn," I said. "Back then."

My father shrugged. "That's all I meant," he said. "We weren't thrashing around the jungle like a bunch of idiots."

"Joe Powers told a different story," my mother said to my father. Then, to me, "Joe was in the Pacific war, on those islands. . . ."

"Corregidor, Iwo Jima," my father said. "But hell, Joe was always a little melodramatic anyway."

A silence passed; we looked at our plates. My father swirled what was left of his iced tea. The ice cubes rang in the glass.

"Maybe somebody knows what's going on over there." My father sighed. "You wouldn't know it from reading the papers, though, I'll tell you."

My mother stacked the dinner plates and asked if we wanted coffee.

"Sounds good," I told her.

My father nodded, watched as my mother moved away, into the kitchen. When she was gone he leaned toward me saying, "One thing about the service. You have your fun." He looked at me, in possession of secrets.

"You know what I mean," he said, smiling. "One time I even shared a rubber. You believe that? No shit. Me and this kid from Tulsa, Oklahoma—Ronnie Bills, I even remember his name—me and Bills and this Mexican girl in the backseat of a rented car. We were on a weekend pass in San Diego, must've been the summer of 'forty-three. Bills went first, gets out and takes off the rubber, empties it out, and gives it to me. Christ." My father was laughing. "What the hell. I mean there we were, one rubber between us and the señorita hot to trot."

My mother turned into the dining room with coffeepot and cups on a tray. My father's laughter subsided and I smiled with the story and he sighed.

"Well," he said, "I guess we did some crazy things back then."

My mother glanced at him as she filled the cups and handed them to us.

"You know, though? What I really loved about those days?" My father stirred sugar into his coffee. "This'll sound strange, maybe, but what I really loved was the music. Really. Benny Goodman, Harry James, Artie Shaw. Glenn Miller. I saw 'em all."

My mother smiled, holding the coffee cup close to her lips. "Your father was quite the dancer," she said.

My father said, "Your mother and I won some dance contests. Jitterbugging. Fox-trots."

"Spotlight dances," my mother said. "I loved those."

"You did those at kind of half speed," my father told me. "You had to be good, couldn't snow the judges with a lot of flailing around and throwing your partner in the air. You had to have a little grace. Of course, I had one hell of a partner." My parents beamed at each other, and my father said, "There was one night. . .the Palladium?"

"You're thinking about Roseland," my mother said.

"Roseland, right." He nodded. "Who was the judge? Some movie star."

"Betty Grable."

My father turned to me. "Your mother and I did an encore dance right up on the bandstand, Glenn Miller playing right behind us."

It was good to have my parents preoccupied with their past, enjoying themselves. I asked if they remembered the steps.

My father grinned. "What do you think? Give the boy a demonstration?"

"I don't know." My mother put her coffee cup on its saucer. "We had a pretty complicated routine."

My father pushed back from the table. "I'll bet we remember every move," he said, and stepped into the adjoining room.

I could hear him flipping through his record collection, sliding albums in and out as my mother said, calling in to him, "It's been years since I even thought about those days. . ."

"Got it!" my father yelled. My mother and I went into the sitting room and he was moving the recliner against a wall. He went to the stereo and set the needle down, and the sound of Glenn Miller's orchestra filled the room and my parents came together to move easily, backing around each other, turns, half turns. My mother swung inside his arms, whirled out; they turned and smiled, looking like the song sounded: supple, in touch with every corner of the room, good-humored and well mannered but ready for anything.

My sisters ran in when they heard the music and danced together, imitating my parents, cavorting and giggling. My parents rode into the music and as the song ended they fell into each other, laughing, my father flushed and panting. "Guess I'm not in the shape I was," he said, patting his belly.

My sisters chased out of the room as my mother leaned on one arm of the recliner, hands on her knees.

"Hey," my father wheezed, "we're still OK, y'know?"

"Well." My mother winked at me. "Not bad."

"Maybe," I said, "I could have the next dance?" My mother smiled, flattered. "By all means. The spotlight dance?"

"Absolutely," I said.

My father put on Harry James doing *September Song* and I placed my left hand in the small of my mother's back, and lifting her left hand in my right I stood poised a moment before we moved off into a box step. My mother looked away from my face.

I said, "I'll be OK."

Her eyes misted and she held her smile in place. "You take care," she said. "Wherever they send you."

"I'll be fine."

"You better be."

"Promise. "

Her smile never wavered. "All right," she said. "I believe you."

8

I said goodbye to Mary on the floor of her parents' basement, a universe of slow heat and half-light, our bodies turning and exquisite. We used television to conceal the sounds of lovemaking and moved in late whispers, as if we could find a private arc of time and live there, protected, in the grip of salvation. Inside her I was desperate and transfixed and believed she must surely feel the same behind her closed eyes. Afterward she would remember things, vagrant moments from years before, the shape of a particular tree on an uncle's farm, the peculiar death of a distant relative, something somebody had said and everybody had forgotten except her. She would tell me the stories as if she was possessed by the memories and I would listen, afraid we were aimless children with no real knowledge of any sort of world, at sea with our own lives.

She told me she was terrified for me, that she might never see me again.

I said I could go somewhere else, Germany maybe.

No, she had told me. They're sending you to Vietnam. And you know they are.

I rolled onto my back and looked at the ceiling. "I don't know anything," I whispered.

"I can't believe we're ending," she said.

"Nothing's ending."

She sat up and spoke with her back to me. "They're taking you away and sending you God knows where and I won't see you. That's an ending." Her voice was flat.

"You'll know where I am. I'll get a leave, I'll come to see you."

Mary continued as if I had said nothing. "I'll be constantly scared you're dead, and I can't live like that."

I looked at her back, the graceful trace of her spine. "Please," I said, "don't do this to me. I can't change anything. I can't help it." I stood and pulled on my jeans.

"I won't wait for you," she said softly. "I mean, I want you back. You know that." She looked down at her body; when she spoke again she was whispering. "But I can't just wait. I'd go crazy. You can't ask me to do that."

I put on my T-shirt, moving as if I were already alone. "I won't ask that," I murmured. I knelt to put on my tennis shoes, laced them. I stood again and told her I would write to her. She began to cry.

9

The air outside the recruiting office was a gash of cold. Windy, overcast. The few of us there stood with hands shoved deep into pockets, moving from foot to foot, waiting for the van that would take us to the induction center. A boy with a motorcycle jacket opened over a torn T-shirt stepped close to the building and tried to light a cigarette against the wind. He went through three matches before I stepped back to shield him and he got the cigarette lit.

"Thanks," he said, squinting at me, smoke whipping away from his face.

A newspaper truck pulled to the curb in front of us. A black boy no more than twelve years old stepped down, dragging a bale of morning editions. He dropped the bale in front of a vending box, pulled wire cutters from a hip pocket and snipped the wire that bound the newspapers. He was a professional: smooth and efficient, unlocking the vending box to take out the day before's leftovers, neatly stacking in fresh papers, sliding a copy into the window rack. Closing the box he gathered wire and newspapers and stepped up into the truck. Gears moaned, the truck lurched away. The black boy stared at us from the open door.

In the window rack of the vending box the close-up face of Lyndon Johnson looked withdrawn and defeated. He was gazing down, leaning his face into his big workman's hand. The headline over the President said MARINES STOPPED NORTH OF SAIGON and, below the headline, *LBJ considers bombing halt.* A side panel had a football player in the air with his hands on the ball and the caption *Redskins clip Oilers in overtime.* A blue van turned the corner and slammed to a halt where the newspaper truck had stood. Our recruiting officer burst out of the van, sharp creases and the smell of aftershave lotion, arranging his garrison cap on a crew-cut skull. He moved briskly to the van's side door, banged it open and turned to face us.

"Gentlemen," he said loudly. "Line up. Right here in front of me, please. One single line."

We shambled into a line.

"Outstanding," the recruiter said. He waited a moment before he spoke again: a memorized speech, and he seemed proud of it. "Gentlemen, you are about to be reborn. You are about to become soldiers, like it or not. May I remind you that these are the last kind words you will ever hear. Best of luck to each and every one of you."

He stepped aside. We filed into the van.

10

The bus, stopped for a light in the middle of a small-town night, stank. We made it stink, all of us packed in. The fat boy next to me was sweating and finally introduced himself, imitating a used-car salesman: loud voice, extended hand, high-school ring. The bus pulled up at the main gate of the Recruit Training Center, military figures vaulting aboard, swinging the aisle, white helmets, guard belts, nightsticks, crisp green trousers stuffed into scrubbed brown leggings with polished gold eyelets. I stood with the others, prodded and herded inside the ornate gates, feet positioned on shoe soles painted on the asphalt at regular intervals, storm troopers between the ranks shouting into ears. Floodlights on. We were marched into a long armory, Drill Hall 31: white squares on blue-fleck linoleum. I was assigned a square. A middle-aged enlisted man appeared and talked like an auctioneer. We were to strip, place our civilian clothes into the cardboard boxes in front of us. We were not to talk. We were not to grabass. We stood at attention nude in 3 A.M. bare-bulb glare, and for thirty seconds the auctioneer looked bored. Then he sighed and said, *You're in the army now.*

11

Training blurred by in a Deep South welter, Spanish moss and magnolia in swamps, drill instructors born out of the flat sun and hostile towns. There was a battery of written tests at scarred schoolroom desks; one by one, soldiers were led out of the room as they reached the part of the test that defied them. When I finished I was taken away to an office where an aging sergeant ran a red pencil over my answer sheet and asked if I'd like to be a medic. Wear a white suit he told me, care for the sick.

I did not answer.

He shrugged and said it was good duty any way you looked at it. People took care of you, looked out for you. Half the time you're in the rear, made in the shade.

I asked about the other half. He shrugged again and said I'd be beating the bush with an infantry company. But, he added, at least I could die a hero.

I asked him what my choices were. For the first time since I came into the office he looked at me, and he smiled gently. He told me that in this man's army there were no choices.

12

The pilot announced that the smudge of coastline moving toward us was the Republic of Vietnam.

Vietnam framed by airplane porthole and haze and first light: the plane banked, turned, for a moment was adrift, leveled out, and the coastline was on the other side of the aircraft, pure green into pure blue, innocent, mysterious, dreaming into the sun.

IN-COUNTRY

1

First look: sandbags and fog. And quiet. As if the fog itself were the carrier of silence easing among us, touching us, loving our faces. Hundred-pound sandbags stacked fifteen high and four deep until life itself was a simple connection between sacks of dirt and the mudhole ring inside them where we talked and ate and slept.

"No, really, man," Linderman told me, talking quietly. "This is what she said. Her exact fucking words. She will wait for me, and there will be no other guys in between. Not unless she gets word I ain't coming back." Linderman looked out on the fog. "God forbid I buy the farm in this shithole."

"You got any smokes?"

He seemed relieved. "Got some Salems. You can cut the filters off if you want."

"No problem."

We crouched behind the sandbags, lit cigarettes where a match flame could not be seen. Against the perimeter, mortar fire started again, booming distantly.

"How many you think's out there in them hills?" Linderman asked me.

I shrugged, flicked an ash. "Captain Bowers heard something like twenty thousand," I said.

"Jesus fucking Christ."

"Maybe more, is what he was saying. Nobody knows for sure."

"You think they mean to overrun us?"

I drew on the cigarette, blowing a mouthful of smoke between us, and said, "So your ladyfriend says she'll wait for you?"

Linderman nodded slowly, looking at me soberly. "That's what she told me," he said.

2

"I had a cat once when I was a kid," Linderman said.

My field glasses were trained into the hills. The shelling had stopped. I saw nothing but the furrowed green textures of mountainside forest. It was nearly six o'clock. Tuesday. An ordinary time in America, I thought: my mother and father sitting down to dinner with my sisters. My older brother and his wife going out for hamburgers.

Linderman said, "Strange how much I loved that cat."

I lowered the field glasses and looked at Linderman. He was crouched inside our sandbag ring, gazing at the ground. I asked him what made him think of his cat.

Linderman shook his head. "I don't know," he said.

I slid to the ground, back against the sandbags.

"The strangest thing," Linderman said, "is that I didn't know how I felt about that cat until it was gone. Then there I was, crying my goddam eyes out, sitting on the edge of the bed, going crazy my mother told me, pounding the mattress and all."

"Well," I said, "you know, you were a kid. Those kind of things mean a lot when you're a kid."

Linderman looked at his boots.

"So what happened to your cat?"

Linderman shrugged. "Got lost," he told me. "Stolen. Wandered off." He shrugged again.

"Know what I was thinking about?" I said. "I was thinking about how there's no time in this place."

Linderman stared at me.

"Really, it's six o'clock, dinnertime; back home everybody's sitting down to eat. Then they'll watch the news, kick back, but they'll know what time it is, where they are, what they're supposed to be doing. Here, it doesn't matter. There's no such thing as time. No beginning, no ending, no in-between. Just living."

"Until we aren't," Linderman said.

I looked at the ground for a moment and then said, softly, "Come on, man."

"Like my old cat. We're all just here until we're not here anymore, right?"

"Hey," I said, "you don't know about your cat. You say he just wandered off. Took a walk. Went to the Bahamas."

Linderman nodded. "That's what we ought to do. Walk away from this shit."

"You know, Linderman, you're forgetting Sergeant Queen's cardinal rule."

"Yeah?"

"Rule number one: nobody dies. You remember?"

Linderman laughed quietly. "Fucking Queen," he said. "He told me that when I came on board. He said maybe some people go away, disappear, you don't see them around anymore, but nobody ever dies. Everybody's somewhere."

Linderman looking at the ground, still laughing, and I smiled too, and I said, "Now, really, Corporal Linderman, you got to remember Queen's rule."

When Linderman looked up at me laughing, his eyes were lit with tears. He said, "OK, nobody dies. Not even cats."

I grinned. "Absolutely," I said.

3

You got a girl back in the world?

The oldest opener, a man heard it everywhere in-country. Some carried wallet-size pictures or graduation shots. Some told stories of how fine it was or was going to be. I had a picture but never showed it to anyone. I used to believe the energy of our every moment—Mary's and mine—lived in that picture of her face, every touch we shared, every private murmur. I had decided it was a charm. My personal good luck piece. If anybody looked at that picture, if I was casual with it, my protection would be lost. A magic at risk. That's how I felt.

Those were the early days in-country. I became less dramatic as time passed. The picture of Mary finally disintegrated in my always-wet hip pocket. I went for it one day, it came out in pieces.

4

"So anyway," Linderman was saying, "we go in this liquor store, it's maybe like two in the morning, all-night liquor store, right? So you know, we're just kids, out on the night and messing around, not a goddam thing to do, and we're thinking we need something to drink. I mean, we've already polished off a couple bottles of Mad Dog Twenty-Twenty between the three of us and we're drunk enough anyways. For kids anyways. And anyway there's only one of us eighteen, old enough to buy a bottle, right? So me and Jackie Franco, we're both underage, we're in this store and our buddy, the guy that's eighteen, he's a little behind us, locking the car or something, right? So we're just looking around, you know, I mean, what do we know from liquor? Store full of the shit and we're probably gonna buy a couple pints of Thunderbird or something, but anyway we're just walking around, talking, bullshitting, and the guy at the counter asks us, you know, big voice, full of authority, Can I help you boys? So Jackie shrugs, waves his hand at the door, says something like we're waiting for a friend. So the guy running the place, old Italian guy, bald head except for these two or three hairs he's got combed down into place, he says Well you can do your waiting somewheres else. And Jackie says But our buddy's coming right in, he's right behind us. And the old Italian guy says This look like the goddam bus station? Go wait somewheres else. Well, I guess we don't move fast enough—I mean, I can see Bobby coming across the lot, he's almost at the door—and the old wop, you ready for this? The old fart pulls a gun on us! No shit. He's got a pistol out and holding it on us and he's saying how we better walk and all, and he's nervous as shit, you know, and about this time Bobby hits the door and stands there a minute, looking at all this, then he says, What the hell is going on? But the old wop is worked up now, he tells us to take a fucking walk, and Bobby goes straight over to the old guy—Bobby was always one real cool son of a bitch—and puts his face up real close to the gun. You know, I'm thinking, Jesus Christ, Bobby! but he's looking at that gun and then he looks at us and then he looks back at the old guy and he starts laughing! And I don't know what the fuck is going on, right? And Bobby says Hey guys, know what? This gun here probably cost about a dollar ninety-eight down to the toy store. And the old guy lets the gun drop, looking disgusted as all get out, and me and Jackie go up there and sure enough. Fucking thing's a toy! Old dude's gonna blow us out of the store with a toy gun. Can you believe that? You know, though, funny thing, we got to be good friends with that old guy. I mean, we ended up going in there all the time, he got all our Saturday night business, we were always laughing, jiving him, you know, about that little toy pistol. He made us promise never to tell anyone, though. Said he'd had to use it a time or two, said it worked both times. So, you know, we said Hey, no problem, right? The secret rests with us. Swear to God. Turns out this guy has a heart attack one night when someone really did rob the place. Weird thing. He was probably going for his toy but was so goddam scared his heart went out on him. He was old and all, but still, weird kind of thing. We missed him. We all went to his funeral up to Little Shepherd. I still think about him, you know? I mean, here I am, corporal in the crotch, and these guns I'm packing sure ain't no goddam toys and if we're stuck in this motherfucking valley much longer I'll probably get so old I'll die of a heart attack too. You know, that old guy was always giving me a load of shit about the nobility of the armed forces, the importance of sacrifice, of serving your country, all that shit. Man, if he only knew. If he only fucking knew."

5

The tent flap lifted from outside. The MP came in, watching us and saying, "You cocksuckers got nothin' but cake."

Howard continued to lay down cards. I was in a hammock to the rear with a month-old Time reading how Jackie Onassis was harassed by an enterprising photographer always trying to catch her in the bathroom or sunning in the nude.

The MP turned and said on the way out, "You boys got a shipment."

Howard stood, stretched, picked up his coffee cup, and started for the flap. "You coming?" he called back, so I swung out of the hammock and followed.

Howard stood with the MP at the rear of a military police van. "Check out this shit," he said to me.

"Musta run over a mine," the MP said. "You shoulda seen the jeep." I climbed into the van: shoveled bodies like piles of old hose. One Vietnamese man, a prisoner, had lost his right arm and his pants. A sergeant looked like he was sleeping. A decapitated lieutenant's head had rolled to the front of the van where it stuck, looking at me. "Let's move this inside," I called out, my voice clouding in front of me, and I leaned for support and my hand went through the sergeant's shirt into his gut that was still warm and the darkness of him froze around my hand, jerking awake from a nightmare, pushing my arm out, into the night, folding back a sleeve to reach blind into black, acidic water, his body talking between my fingers, sending one short gut moan for the bad light the explosion let in, and I lifted my hand out covered with his blood and shit.

I looked at Howard. It was raining into his coffee cup, coffee splashing to his thumb and wrist. "Man," the MP said, "you shoulda seen that jeep."

6

Lifting off from near Hue, Wednesday dawn. I was born on a Wednesday, this time of day, laborers rolling to catch the alarm, blinking in the sudden vacant spot of the bedside lamp.

There is a recurring notion of violin music in the dark. I can't trace it: a thread of what's recalled or forgotten. Looking at everything I can see, sun rising out of the Pacific, transcendental magenta and scarlet, rain forest rowing north into a settled haze and mountain, mythological, azure and green. Me at the open port of a helicopter dreaming the view of more than one river at once.

7

The hamlet was ordinary enough, kids chasing us for candy and powdered chocolate and cigarettes, their parents silhouetted by the half dark of doorways. Near the end of the hamlet an old woman was squatting with a skinny, panting dog. We were nearly by when she spoke, Vietnamese, to no one in particular. The lieutenant looked back, around the edge of the column to see the woman, then halted the platoon. He walked within a few feet of her. She did not move.

The lieutenant abruptly shouted "VC?"

She stared at his face.

The lieutenant called Corporal Howard out; Howard knew some Vietnamese. He leaned close to Howard, an illusion of secrets. "Did you hear what she said, corporal?"

Howard looked at the old woman and did not answer. The lieutenant asked again, louder, more authority, "What she say, Corporal Howard?"

I watched a spider touch its way along the sill of the hootch doorway behind the old woman. She squatted and stared at the bridge of the lieutenant's nose.

"Well, sir," Howard said. "She called us. . .uh, dogs, something like that. Maybe like go to hell, something like that."

"Yeah, well." The lieutenant nodded. "You ask her what she knows about Charlie." The lieutenant spit Texas-style, turned sideways looking into the distance, job delegated. Howard hesitated, said something to the woman, and she broke a semi-toothed betel-nut grin. Then she laughed, full-throated, head back.

The lieutenant studied her, reached to unbuckle his holster flap. "Perhaps an understanding can be arrived at," he said, "as to just who the dogs are." He withdrew the .45, clicked the safety off. The blood drained away from my eyes: I stepped toward him, slowly, called his name as calmly as I could. He was leveling the pistol, aiming. He spoke as quietly as I did. "Back in formation, soldier."

Holding the pistol in both hands, arm's length, he fired.

The dog's head turned inside out, splashing the woman, its body bursting like a dropped sack.

8

Dear Mary,

I am enclosing a photograph of myself. The dark stains on my shirt are mostly sweat, a little blood. Not my own, so not to worry. The chain around my neck carries the St. Christopher medal you sent me: even though I am not religious its power seems immense. I wear it with the embossed tags that will identify me in the event of my death. Please excuse my lack of expression. Forgive the look of fatigue and dull hatred you see in my eyes. The thousand yard stare somebody here called it, and I thought I didn't know what that meant, but here it is, reaching back in my eyes.

The weapon in my right hand is a pirated Ithaca Magnum-10 shotgun, gas-operated, semi-automatic, a full-choke barrel sawed down to ten inches for ease in single-hand handling at close quarters. It was captured from a North Vietnamese officer, later presented to me as a gift.

The bulge in my left hip pocket is a soggy paperback edition of the poems of Emily Dickinson.

Such things live together here, poetry and shotguns. Alive and well in a single body.

The photograph is candid and was not taken with my permission, but once given to me its silence loomed. I send it on not to frighten or disturb but to confirm my existence beyond the transience of my words.

9

Memory rode out of its past like a killer on the run, the trance for hire, blues in half tones sung against morning's first light. I would wake to a hand reaching toward me in front of a whispered voice I could not quite hear, and it never mattered if it was only a dream or real as waking up with a start in the warehouse of the night, alive in the jungle mind, light leaking through the seams. I would run my hand across my head, feeling the feel of my body after most of the night on the ground, and morning's first light was always gray before it was blue; the platoon would be up, spitting, blowing noses. I was reasonably good at heating C-rats without burning them: stirred water into the blank pudding of canned ham-and-egg, turned it to muck, dumped in some of the hot sauce my mother airmailed me, kept it all over low flame. The lieutenant would already be moving through the platoon, general harassment. Part of a lieutenant's job, Sergeant Queen always said.

Got an onion out of the gas-mask bag I kept them in, chopped a little into the heating ham-and-eggs. I traded the mask for onions in a hamlet we patrolled. After a while nobody gave a shit for their protective gear.

10

The little Vietnamese man shadowed the hootch doorway, walked carefully out into a circle of sun, arms straight up. The little man held his arms up and looked at his feet and stood in the circle of sun.

There was a slow wind, birds clacking, monkeys cawing, the wrapped surrender of the little man in his halo.

One soldier spilled a plate of food screaming Goddammit, hold it! the little man's feet clearing earth, one arm laid out in the air, chest jerking perforations, body sailing backward, falling in the shadow of his doorway.

The lieutenant jogged around a corner and up to the hootch. "Nice work," he said. "This little bastard is no doubt VC. Gotta be. Write it up, Gunny."

The lieutenant dragged the little man back into the sun circle, kicked the turned-out corpse like he was checking a tire. He opened his Swiss Army knife, sawed off the man's left ear. Blood squirt. "Son of a bitch," he said into the dead face. The lieutenant stood up, called out, "Which one of you good buddies got a camera?"

11

Hey, kid, how about this postcard? Thought you might like a look at the old town right about now. Where the hell are you? Sorry I didn't see you before you left. Hot as Hades here but what's new about that? Not enough rain and the Ohio farmers bitching about profits down and how they can't make their tractor payments—same old story. Mainly want to say sorry we didn't get together before you left and we will when you get back and you're not forgotten here with us. Your grandma sends all her love and BE CAREFUL. Can't say it enough. Don't get much room to write on these things do you? Love, Grandad.

12

Field-stripping weapons: cleaning our pieces, Queen taking down his M-14 as I spread my pistol in parts on a canvas ground cloth, an AMT Combat Government model, .45 caliber semi-automatic: 7-shot clip, 5-inch barrel. All stainless steel construction, target trigger, adjustable combat sights and less than two pounds. I traded a half kilo of marijuana for the gun from an armory sergeant in Pleiku. Queen admired the pistol, more elegant than standard issue, and I offered to sell it to him. Shit, I don't need it, I told him, grinning. And he laughed, saying, You might, bro, you just might. Tell you what, he said, we get outta here in one piece, that little gun'll be mine. Deal, I told him. When we get outta here.

13

Six months into the tour Private First Class Clovis Taggett of Simpson, Arkansas, shot and killed an old woman advancing into a paddy. Nobody actually saw him fire. We were eating under a copse of banyan, dropped to the ground and saw Taggett on the lip of the dike, lone figure standing black against the sunlight. His rifle was still poised.

The old woman continued to advance, moving away from us. Her arms went up, a hallelujah gesture, and she fell face first into the water. The splash shone brilliant in the light. She was about forty yards out.

"The enemy," Taggett said flatly. "Trying to escape."

"Jesus," the lieutenant said. "Eat your goddam lunch. We're mounting out in fifteen."

Taggett slung his piece, wandered back to the group, sat down and slumped against an exposed tree root. The lieutenant, crouched beside me, resumed his lunch. I looked at Taggett a moment before I turned and said to the lieutenant, "He lost it. He just snapped."

"Happens all the time, man," the lieutenant said around a mouthful of beans. "You've been here long enough to know that."

I looked again at Taggett, who was staring at the ground, empty-faced. "We gotta get him out of here," I told the lieutenant. "He's a medevac."

"He'll be all right," the lieutenant said.

I took a long breath. "The guy's shooting old women for laughs," I said, "and you're telling me he'll be all right."

The lieutenant looked up at me, letting his spoon drop into the bean can. "He'll be all right, man. So give it a rest." He frowned at me before going back to eating. I turned back to Taggett, still sitting on the tree root, looking like a moody child. I stood and threw what was left of my rations into the dirt, kicking dust over the moist mound. Out in the paddy on the surface of the water shining in sunlight the old woman's corpse was adrift. A boy was shouting at her, and began to wade out.

14

Monsoon. Rain five weeks, complete in itself. Nothing beyond it, dreams locked in water. Deadfall from flat sky, constant hiss into mud and drum against tents. Four-thirty A.M. A thickness washing the chest and legs for days.

Mud-suck boots onto elevated wood-slat platform of chow tent. Bare hanging light bulbs. Ambulance driver sitting alone at a bench, mug of coffee cooling as he paged through a glossy magazine. Only a few others in line for the powdered eggs and cold, undercooked bacon. Water seeping into the boards, mildew eating canvas. I sat down across from the driver. At one page he turned the magazine around for me to see. A young girl, maybe fifteen, squatting in full-page color. Her breasts were new and her smile was a benign yearbook grin. She was holding a foot-long dildo in one hand, fingering herself with the other.

He pulled the magazine back and continued flipping pages. He showed me the cover: two teenagers in a sixty-nine with black flags covering the important places. He finished the cold coffee and rolled the magazine into a hip pocket and stomped out.

A chopper came down into the LZ, rotors cutting a space in the rain. The weight that started in my stomach grew in my lungs like a tide.

Contact near Fire Base Louise, no survivors. We bagged the captain and the legless lance corporal and called Motor T to get the bodies to Graves. I went out behind the tent, feeling it all in slow motion. I was forgetting every detail, could not remember my name. Nausea swam behind my ribs and I could not remember my name.

15

Queen said, "The man has got to go."

We were in a bunker, sharing a joint on a wind-locked night.

I said, "You out of your mind or what? That's called murder where I come from."

Queen rolled his eyes, drawing in a lungful, holding, swallowing smoke, blowing it out through clenched teeth, talking with the smoke. "What you think we be doing, my man, all day every day? That just a popgun you packing?" He spit a seed on the concrete floor, handed me the joint. An ember flew, flared an arc.

"Besides," Queen went on, "that dude gonna get us all wasted anyway."

"What I'm saying," I said, "is there's one thing and there's another. And you're talking about the other."

Queen looked at me red-eyed and said, "What I'm saying is I'm gonna blow that peckerwood into China. He be arriving in Peking in small pieces.'"

Queen and I sat, alone in the bunker, looking at each other, looking. A rain began to spatter, into the mud, hissing. Then the full roar of downpour.

"I mean it, man," Queen said.

"Let it go," I said.

"New guys get you killed, bro."

I studied the glow of the joint between my thumb and finger, and I said, "Let's just hit him over the head when he gets out of hand."

Queen began to laugh.

And I began to laugh. And we laughed and I dropped the joint as I tried to pass it back to Queen, watching Queen howl as the rain roared against the bunker and into the jungle as we rolled on the concrete floor gasping, short of breath and wasted, two soldiers afraid for their lives and laughing.

16

Months passed before the second card from my grandfather. The picture side depicted the gleaming suspension bridge that could be seen from his kitchen windows, CARTER RIGNEY BRIDGE, AN ENGINEERING TRIUMPH, with the message below the legend, six weeks out of date.

My grandmother was dead.

Killed when the car she was riding in—driven by her youngest daughter—left the road near Salem, West Virginia, and slammed into the side of Big Harper Mountain. My grandfather went through the details like a newscaster.

I sat against a sandbag retaining wall, turning the postcard to the picture side, back to the message side. Read it again. Queen sat a few feet away, opening a package from his mother, no shirt and black skin glistening in the open sun.

"My grandmother's been killed," I said.

Queen looked up, studying me. "I'm sorry to hear, man," he said. He studied a moment longer, and said, "I really am. You close to her?"

"Car wreck," I murmured.

"Goddam cars, man." Queen shook his head. "Put away more people than we do in this piss-ant war."

I felt remote, too small for the sky.

"You wanna be left alone or anything?"

"I'm OK," I said. "Gotta be, right?"

Queen said, "I guess."

I asked Queen what his mother had sent him, and he went back to his package.

Eight months in-country. Five to go.

17

Dear Mary,

Coming down the road in the fog and everyone here is a ghost, changed by mist and a haze of rain, and I think of coming back to this valley ten years from now, twenty years from now, seeing the past I belong to: we will all be here still, in this moment we must live and keep living, walking down the road talking, laughing, complaining, wishing, finding the way to a latrine, to a card game, to the mail drop. Hearing, out of sight, the sounds of other conversations, of weapons being cleaned, jeep engines idling and waiting for officers moving from one useless briefing to another. It will be like it is now, walking down the road with the rest, except I will seem more real, I will hear the inside of my heart moving, the rush of blood through the chambers of my heart. I will remember the smell of this rain as clearly as I am breathing it now: this is the way it is with ghosts. We look at our own hands and even in this fog we are real as ever, veins branching, tendons rising and moving, fingers clenching and spreading and feeling, simply alive with a whisper of rain and the hours rolled into a map.

18

Night patrol, in a hamlet marked Blueville 5 on military topo-
graphical maps. The platoon securing a village supposedly a VC
stronghold. I was holding in a cleared area with the rest of the
unit closing down around me, my partner gone to pull his radio
off the command jeep, and I leaned against a grass bale hearing
pigs root and grunt from some other part of the settlement,
hearing the voices of women, children crying, soldiers shouting.
Across from my position the open door of a hootch gaped black
and I heard movement in the doorway, a soft scraping. I could
see nothing. I felt for my flashlight, remembered I left it with
my pack next to the radio on the command jeep, and there was
another noise, a dry click. I called my partner's name, and again
a sound in the doorway, the scratch of footfall on straw, unmis-
takable. There was no cover around me. The jungle a few yards
to my rear. I called for help, going to one knee saying to the
doorway, in English, *Anyone there?* My voice was a horrified rasp,
barely audible, the sound of it frightening me more than I
already was. I unholstered my service pistol, released the safety,
thinking I could turn into the jungle and cover the doorway
until the platoon swept this far in another thirty seconds.

Then I thought: Unless that is what is expected of me, and I brought the pistol up in both hands, elbows locked, and said, in Vietnamese as I was trained to do, *Identify yourself or I will shoot.* Silence. Another rustle in the doorway. Silence.

I fired the pistol into the center of the darkness, the powder burst sparking a clean light that seemed to arc forward from the barrel's tip and back in again. There was the .45's short open roar, echo crushing in behind it, empty air sucked into the vacuum. A fire team was suddenly all around me, submachine guns trained and flamethrowers cocked. The lieutenant turned a high-intensity beam into the doorway, and I saw the man.

He was blown off his feet by the blast and his body was in the distinctive scarecrow disarray that instant death brings. I was still on one knee ten yards from the doorway, and I stood and walked to the body. A Vietnamese man, my age or younger, unarmed, alone, with nothing on but his traditional black silk pants.

I had shot him in the face.

BONE BLOOD

1

In the evening we were quiet, sitting in base camp in damp T-shirts in the damp air looking out to the perimeter. We were home from an extraction, the sort of mission you mount out for having dismissed all regret and second thought. We went out, two gunships up front and me behind on the evacuation chopper, pilots fired on the adrenaline wail, hitting their fists together as we waited for the go. We brought home a long-range reconnaissance patrol that had infiltrated the Cambodian line. December twenty-fourth and sweat dripped from my eyebrows and the salt stung my eyes and I felt as if I were short of breath, squinting into too much silver light.

It was clean flying in open skies, verdant unbroken jungle below. We were up nearly twenty minutes when the pilot waved me forward. *Hot pursuit,* he shouted over the rotor roar. *Going in under fire.* I saw the spout of emerald phosphorus, smoke pluming out of the jungle about two miles ahead. The gunships, tiny in the distance, banked starboard as if they were tied together, angled out, adjusted their slip, and pumped three rockets apiece into the jungle floor. We continued to close as pockets of flame blew silently out of the forest, erupting one beside the other. A moment later the shock waves reached us, distant thunder that might have been imagined. The pilot was shouting into his headset; ahead, the LZ clearing was visible. Smoke rose and dispersed on a fresh wind. The pilot swung the chopper around on its axis and as we rotated I saw the front range of trees on the enemy flank charred and blasted from the rockets, here and there in flames. Automatic weapons fire whanged off our armor plate as the aircraft fell, our pickups breaking from underbrush before we touched down, dragging wounded and dead, pushing bound prisoners ahead of them. I watched a soldier—another man on his shoulders in a fireman's carry—work his way into the elephant grass, trying to run and limping, halfway out when his chest opened in a bloody gush and he went down in a wet heap with the man on his back. The cockpit glass shattered in a white spray; the pilots seemed to take no notice. My ears roared and head pounded as I squatted in the helicopter doorway. The dead man's comrades stepped over him, running, stumbling, and we began to bring them aboard. A soldier shoved a man into the hatch and ran back for the dead, dragging two at a time by the boots, and somewhere behind me the world exploded—slammed me onto my back—but when I took a breath I was clear, strangely calm, the shell of the helicopter intact around me. I got up, went back to work, did my job, and in the evening we sat quietly, reading, writing letters, smoking, sharing around gifts of food or magazines that had come as Christmas gifts from the families at home. I sat on a canvas stretcher, back against a supply chest, looking into an invisible distance, not reading or writing or smoking or eating or talking, stunned by a luck of the draw that was weak as the past or future, and it was as if I were simply earning my keep, and could only have this much, and tomorrow was never another day.

2

A leg wound, my trouser leg blood-soaked, fabric congealed in muscle and other wounded around me calling out. The gunfire was distant, pulling away like an animal retreating. A gentle rain began and I felt tired, as if I could sleep, hearing the colonel's voice from weeks before, flat monotone reading a Department of Defense memorandum in a sweep debriefing, for our information, he said. Things we should know. Things we would be interested in. We were exhausted, wet, dirty, in shock, sitting in rows. The colonel had congratulated us on a job well done. The Department, he said, had calculated the percentages of engagements we were involved in. He began to read: 7.1 percent were chance engagements, both sides surprised. He adjusted bifocals to look at a very white piece of paper and continued: 8.9 percent, U.S. forces ambush a moving enemy unit. He looked up, grinning, saying, Those are the kind we like, right? Nobody responded and his grin faded and he went on: a moving U.S. unit engages the enemy in a dug-in or fortified position, 17.9 percent. Queen leaned dose to my ear and whispered, *What the fuck is he talking about?* The Colonel read on: 30.4 percent involve organized enemy attacks against U.S. static defense perimeters. Queen said *Organized enemy?* Forget it, I said. On the operation Queen and I had been en route on a midafternoon along Highway Three, Queen driving the jeep, sun-blasted, and we approached a corpse lying in the middle of the road. As we gained on the body we saw it was headless, neck stump a blackened sawtooth. The sun so hot it seemed unnatural and Queen swerved to avoid the body, shouting over the engine, Where the hell's his head? We passed and I shouted back, Gone for a souvenir. Jesus Christ, Queen had yelled, downshifting, You're probably right.

It was raining harder, stinging my cheeks, a rich muddy smell. I was drifting in and out of pain, dreaming, somehow in another time, and it seemed easy to think of the smell of water in other places, the beach at night with an unexpected rain spattering a driftwood fire, Mary's body lit and shadowed, or the way summer rains blew and gushed over the river behind my grandfather's house, veil of haze and chill pushing a wall of August heat across the water's face, and I looked up at the heavy Asian sky knowing how simple it would be to let go, to turn my breath loose, and the world gaped, roared, turned on its side, spinal warp opening vistas into my body, down into my body that was big as the earth. No job for the fainthearted, the colonel had said. Right. But he had never told us how to die. Nobody, I realized, had ever told me how to die. Somewhere, nearer than before, an explosion, a short tight burst. A grenade, and I tried to move my leg. Nothing. I fell back, wet slap on mud, the man next to me belly up in downpour, still alive but probably dying and mumbling in a high-pitched voice, calling to people I did not see. *Sure, baby, I'll tell her,* he was saying, *you can rely on me. Right away, baby. No problem.* He began to sing, a lullaby. Another grenade burst and I tried to move, rolled to crawl and the motion brought an elastic pain that covered me, shut out the sky, took my breath. The rain thundered, mist in the air like mirage shimmer and inside the gush of rainfall I heard the bleat of helicopters. Pain labored the length of my leg, a generous pain, and I wanted to shout at the helicopters, I wanted to stand up and wave my arms and I was cheek-down in mud, falling, a stone through darkness at the limits of the known world falling along the ridges of the last visible horizon, arms pushing against the air rushing into my face, alone in that darkness and falling.

3

Supine on a filthy canvas stretcher I remembered horror movies at the small theater next to the department store in my grandfather's hometown, my terror of a bloody hand reaching for me in the upstairs dark, a blanched and eyeless face suddenly in a third-story window. I remembered the light in 1955, beside the river with autumn rising. An industrial city bone-tired and alone the way depression and war left such places, islands out in America, train town, city of retired conductors and brakemen, farmers whose country died, the displaced middle-aged cranking up textile and chemical plants along the river, bored pawnbrokers, damp housewives in sack dresses desperate over stoves, managers of five-and-dimes. A small item appeared in the local obituaries: James Dean was dead behind his steering wheel.

I touched my bandage, wet, the palm print where I was seized when the heat came down. I had dreamed of violence, of injury. And there were other dreams: days of snow. Miles and seasons from where I was and warm inside me. A room in a huge old house like a painting, winter walking away from the windows. There was music, an embodiment. I woke up when the pleasure began to hurt in my chest.

And there were dreams of flying.

4

I was ascendant.

With the sense of levitation the pain was subdued, quieter. And when someone screamed or a helicopter landed the pain rose to fill me deadfall to gasping contact, diffusing to own my legs.

Mary in her mother's pink convertible at the curb and my father smiling easily in the cavalier sophistication that leaned on the mantel Errol Flynn style, saying Sure, have a good time for me. So we drove and drove, gentle into the sundown wind past the high school and stadium and the outdoor markets to the highway where Mary opened the night, her hair standing straight behind her, not another car in sight. She took me to a golf course with mist collecting over the water traps: we walked out of sight of the car and sat down at the top of a long fairway.

We kissed with a determination, a natural ache, and Mary pulled away, looking at me evenly, drawing down the straps of her summer dress.

Driving home I watched the sky slide over, purple air and the memory of her breasts stippled from night cold, the kind of private event that might save me, a thing I could own free and clear.

My stomach began to undulate, to fold in its glove of muscle when the pain used up my legs. I tried to call out.

5

My father was still awake in his tartan bathrobe. Watching the eleven o'clock news. He asked if Mary and I had a nice drive. When the news signed off he heaved up from the olive-green recliner, pulling his robe tighter. I remembered the spray of Mary's headlights over a country road as if I were no longer in the car, as if I had been a boy standing alone on the side of the night, watching the points of light approach, flash, slowly flow back into the darkness inside my head.

My father stood for a few minutes waiting to see what the late show would be: *Flying Leathernecks; Thirty Seconds over Tokyo; Back to Bataan; Run Silent, Run Deep.* Hell of a time, my father said, we had with the Japs. They just about did us in.

I wanted to remember but the details swam: I watched the headlights approach, circles of intense light out of a black distance, converging, roaring, blinding sheen, and I know what I heard, capsized insight, the day I was leaving my mother crying and my father shaking my hand, saying *All of us have a duty that's more important than ourselves.*

6

Through-and-through shrapnel wounds with fractured bone. I was airlifted to a staging hospital, underwent surgery, debridement, sewing, plastering. *Not too bad*—my surgeon nodded from the end of the bed—*all things considered. Coulda been a lot worse.*

One afternoon in the hospital we heard an announcement. Bob Hope was touring in-country, entertaining the troops. The announcement came just after a general stopped in to award a Silver Star. I was asked to sit at the soldier's bedside in a wheelchair, an audience, the witness. The soldier's head was a white swath stained yellow and green at the temples, eyes staring flat as stones from a window in the tapes. I had overheard one of the surgeons on rounds, looking down at the bandages.

Brain's gone, he said. *All we can do is wait him out.*

The general's aide read the citation about meritorious action in the face of a hostile enemy. Citations always told the story in one hundred words or less, small translations of how lives ended on bleached afternoons along riverbanks or inside the nights, suffocating in rain. The soldier with the bandaged head had escaped a mortared bunker but returned to reclaim a burning corporal, killing four or five of the enemy with knife and side arm on the way back in. He sustained his wounds on the crawl out, taking shrapnel in the head and shoulders but moving on with the burning man on his back.

The man he rescued, I was told by those who were there, was dead by the time they gained cover. They were both in flames.

The medal rested in a case lined with scarlet velvet, was opened in front of the soldier's eye window, and he stared through the box lid, into the bed across the aisle, into the next world. I wheeled slowly back to my cot. As the entourage moved out, the general's aide stepped to one side in the doorway and announced that Bob Hope and company would be at the hospital in the coming week. Mr. Hope was coming to cheer us up, he said. The aide read prepared copy typed onto an index card. We would all be expected to attend the performance. He read on about classic humor, beautiful girls, and a special musical guest. Then he turned and was gone.

All of us, all of us who could, watched the doorway in a lengthening silence; all of us, bandaged, minus limbs, minus eyes, in traction, in body casts, in wheelchairs, on crutches, we watched the vacant doorway. The soldier with the Silver Star continued to stare into the same square of empty space. His medal glinted in its case, with a copy of the citation on the bedside table.

I heaved up to my cot and lay down and looked at the water-stained ceiling, listening to helicopters coming and going, smelling the mud and sweat. My mind seemed useless to me, an old engine riding into a backwash, lost in the world I had called home. I sat on the side of the bed to reach for some stale C-ration chocolate I had saved, and I was unable to cry, or speak, or move.

7

A chaplain made rounds while I was on convalescent status. Usually he only nodded; now he was pulling a folding chair to my bedside, pointing to the book I was reading. A paperback mystery from the hospital library. A black stamp defaced the worn cover: DONATED BY AMERICAN RED CROSS.

"Good book?"

"Wonderful," I said. "All about murder and deception."

"I see," the chaplain said, sitting down.

There was uneasy silence between us. I put the book aside. "Something I can do for you, Father?"

The chaplain pursed his lips before he spoke. "Your doctor mentioned you might be in the market for somebody to talk to. He thinks your recovery's been a lonely one."

"Hell, no," I said. "A veritable party."

The chaplain crossed his legs, patted one hand on his knee three times, looked away.

I said, "I'm not really in the market for much of anything just now, Father. No offense."

"None taken."

I nodded.

"They have you doped up?"

I smiled, closed my eyes. "Haven't had a thing today," I said.

The chaplain told me he imagined it was hard for a man to say what was on his mind, things being what they were. He was as crisp as his uniform, thin black hair falling away from a receding hairline.

I opened my eyes. "Things being what they are," I said.

"That tremor," the chaplain said. "Your doctor mentioned that. What's that about?"

I reached a pack of cigarettes from under my pillow, offered one to the chaplain.

He declined. "It's no smoking in here," he said.

I swung my casted leg over the bedside, sat up, lit the cigarette.

"So what about that tremor," the chaplain said.

"Anger," I said.

"Anger?"

"Pure and simple."

The chaplain looked confused.

"Terrible anger," I said quietly. "Rage."

"Don't you mean fear? I mean, why should you be angry?"

I stared at him.

"Really," he went on. "Your platoon commander tells me you're a remarkable young man. Courageous. Intelligent. Tough. Your platoon looks up to you. He said they all consider you a good-luck charm."

"Soldiers are superstitious," I said.

"In fact," the chaplain said, "and maybe I'm not supposed to tell you this, but you're being recommended for a very high decoration. For how you handled that situation out near Cu Chi."

I blew smoke, extinguishing the cigarette on the inner wall of a Styrofoam cup. "Father," I said, "I didn't even know what I was doing. I didn't even know who I was shooting at."

The chaplain uncrossed his legs. His shoulder insignia sparkled under the fluorescent bulbs.

"I didn't even see the face of the man I killed," I said. "I was just a terrified guy with a gun."

The chaplain looked at me, and I knew he would not pretend to understand. I had read most of the mysteries in the hospital library and the tremors were subsiding and the cast was due to be removed the next day. I would be pronounced healthy, recovered, able-bodied, fit for duty. I would be returned to my unit. They would be in the bush, I had been told, out on a a search-and-destroy. I could fly out to join them on the supply chopper. Everyone would be happy to see me.

8

Tropical rain, the rain that begins suddenly in downpour, drilled across the face of palm fronds and gushed out of trees, vibrated across my helmet. The firefight ended as suddenly as the rain began and I had given the man I was with two Syrettes of morphine, one in each arm, and laced two battle dressings over his thigh wound, one on top of the other. The blood was still soaking through.

He motioned me closer and I took my helmet off so I could hear him. The rain slowed to a whisper and ran out of my hair and he spoke into my ear: *That's bone blood down there.*

I turned my head to look at him. "You mean did you get hit in the bone?"

"I mean that's marrow blood running out of me now," he said. "You get that kind of bleeding you done for."

"You're going straight out of here," I said. "We're going straight out of here together."

"We may get out of here," he said, "but a man draws bone blood he be bleeding forever." He looked at me, lips drawn tight over his teeth, and said, "He be bleeding forever, you hear me?"

The rain stopped and the forest clicked as water fell into groundcover and we stared at each other, his eyes flickering in disappearing light. Mist filtered, smoke and constant drip. In the distance, the hoarse choke of approaching helicopters.

"Choppers coming," I said. "We're on the way."

"Gonna bleed the rest of my life," he hissed. "Gonna be coming right out of my bones all the rest of my life. You hear what I'm saying?"

I looked at him and the sound of the helicopters grew closer. "I hear what you're saying," I whispered.

9

Waiting for sun. Rain coming. The top sergeant who lost six toes to frostbite and three fingers to a grenade at Cochin Reservoir in Korea said, "Go on out there, fellas, make sure there's none of our guys left out there."

Linderman and I looked out at the hillside from the bunker porthole.

Top said, "We ain't leaving none of our guys out there."

Linderman glanced at me and said, "Yeah, what if we go out there and end up like some of those dudes laying on the ground? You thought of that, Top? I ain't going out there for no goddam stroll."

The Top sat down on a sandbag, sighed, said, "That's what's wrong these days. No goddam cooperation. Trying to run a war with assholes like you. I must really be too old for this shit. Times've changed too much on me."

"Christ," Linderman said, "here we go."

"When I joined the army things were different," the Top said. "Yes sir."

"Top," Linderman said. "You're breaking my heart. You know that?"

The Top reflected. "Probably all you guys on dope," he said. "Can't run a war on dope."

"Shit," Linderman said, "give me a break."

"So we just gonna leave our boys out there? That coulda been you out there, Linderman. Tomorrow it probably will be. So I can just write to your mother, Hey, no sweat, your boy don't care if his body turns to shit out there in no-man's-land."

Linderman moved to the porthole, not responding, looking at the corpses on the hillside.

"We can just let the rats chew on your worthless bones," the Top said, standing up. "So give me a fucking break, Linderman. I'll go out there myself. I'll be damned if I'll leave even one of our guys to rot in that slime." Top turned to me. "Does Linderman give a shit? I ask you."

Linderman was still studying the hillside and spoke without turning around, speaking gently. "Hey, Top, I guess I see how you feel. We'll get 'em. We'll get the job done. Don't you worry 'bout a thing."

The old sergeant squinted into the dense air. "Really," Linderman said. "Don't worry about it. Sit back down. We'll bring 'em home. Every one of 'em."

10

Moonless night on a hill. Faces visible in deep shadow, dream-light. Night sounds: isolated monkey scream in jungle distance, giant cricket, dragonfly whir.

"Jesus." Queen sighed softly. "I'd love a cigarette."

"Yeah," I whispered.

We sat, silent. After a few minutes Queen whispered, "How the hell long we been up here anyway?"

"Who knows?" I said. "Who cares?"

"Who cares?" Queen laughed under his breath, said, "My momma cares, dude. Don't you know that?"

Our intelligence had reported North Vietnamese army activity in the area, moving in our direction. We were dug in, deep cover, waiting. Riflemen stationed prone on the escarpment lip, 360-degree outposting.

"Christ," Queen said, "I don't know if I gotta shit or puke."

"Maybe both," I said.

"Both what?"

"Shit and puke."

A low throaty whistle. The signal. One of the sentries had spotted something, heard something. Something moving. I laid my cheek to the earth, smelling rank wet odor of jungle, each breath roaring, burning in my nose. NVA, I thought. With a rocket launcher they can simply blow us out of our bed. So it occurred to me.

Then I thought: Maybe not NVA. Maybe an animal. Or a lookout so nervous he imagined something. My ear to the earth and a pain in my chest spreading against the moist ground. We lay, and lay, and after a time another whistle like the first. All clear. It was past, whatever it was. Or was not. Or only a wild-eyed point man, another American teenager in the grip of a bad midnight on a hill in a jungle country.

"It's OK man," Queen was whispering to me. I felt his hand on my arm and I kept my ear pressed to the ground, listening to the sound night makes moving inside the earth, on a low hill, in a jungle country.

11

Linderman said, "This is all she wrote I guess."

"Come on."

"Don't bullshit me," Linderman said. "Not now. We've come too far together for you to bullshit me now."

"Take it easy," I said.

"I'm dead and I know it. Only a goddam matter of time."

Linderman's chest was a matted heap of bloody meat: shotgun blast. Close-quarters ambush outside a little buffalo ville, a standoff. Linderman killed the man who shot him.

"Very weird," Linderman said. He was breathless, as if he had run a long distance.

"What's that?"

"Well, you know, sitting here talking like this waiting to die."

"You just might make it through this, you know."

Linderman grinned. "Fucking liar," he said.

I tried to grin back.

"This sucker's starting to hurt. That's strange. It's just starting to hurt."

"Take it easy."

"Hey, fuck you," Linderman said. And grinned again.

I took a breath.

"You hit anywhere?"

"Don't think so," I said. "Don't worry about it."

Linderman grimaced, grabbed at my shirt, opened his mouth wide: blood smeared on his teeth. He choked, gagged; I pushed his head to the side as he vomited blood. He tried to speak. When he did, a whisper. "God, man. Don't let me go."

I cradled his head.

"Strange," Linderman whispered. "I'm young."

"Yeah. We all are."

"I wish I was just gone and didn't have to think about nothing," he said.

I reached behind him, lifting his body off the ground, embracing him. He looked at me, his eyes clear and troubled, and he said, "Now I'm gonna cry. What a goddam thing."

"Go ahead," I said. "I've got you. I'm with you." A call for help from a few yards away, a call for water.

"Hey," Linderman said, "see what you can do over there. Get that man some water."

"Howard can get him," I said.

Linderman said, "It's OK, man. I'll be all right."

"I'll be right back."

"Sure."

I lowered him to the ground; he groaned as I pulled my arms free. The man who wanted water had been hit in the legs, fragmentation spray, Howard working on him when I got there. I let the wounded man sip from my canteen. When I tried to pull away he pushed forward for more, so I left the canteen with him and moved back to Linderman.

And Linderman was dead.

MALARIA

1

An old story. A simple story. The story of a boy lost on a weekend furlough in a small town in the middle of America. I was sitting in the apartment of a woman I met in a bar, lithe woman with blond hair and tortoise-shell glasses, smoking her cigarettes and beginning to understand just what a stranger I really was. She asked questions, trying to spark conversation. *Why are you doing this?* I was drafted. *You could have gone to Canada. You can still go to Canada.* No. I cannot go to Canada. That was never an option.

Bullshit, she said quietly. Don't give me that.

I'm not giving you anything. It's not a simple situation.

Do you believe in what you're doing?

Not particularly.

Well, then?

Well then what?

Why don't you just. . .not go back? What're you doing out there anyway?

Training.

For war?

Most definitely.

So that's what they're doing out there.

I laughed, and said, It's no secret what they're doing out there. They've been doing it out there for years.

I guess so. It's just that nobody talks about it. And I've never met anyone in the. . .military.

We're your basic silent types. We don't mingle.

Oh, right. A legion of Gary Coopers?

High noon. High noon in the rice paddies.

God.

Listen. . .

You're different from what I would have expected. I just can't believe it's not driving you crazy.

I can't change anything. And there are. . .certain pressures. . . family, ideas I've been carrying around. I don't know. It's not simple.

You can come and see me.

Well. We'd better not get into that.

Why not?

I'll be gone in short order. Shipped out.

So?

It just doesn't seem wise. I don't know. . .

Doesn't it. . .I mean the training. . .I mean, how do you do it?

I just do it. I'm there, and I do it.

Doesn't it. . .get to you?

I'm scared to death.

Two doctors at my bedside. The light around them haloed, burned, shimmered. They wore olive-drab combat utilities under their white coats and one said, talking too loud, How's it going, guy? My mouth moved but I had to try a second time to speak before the words came, and I asked: *Malaria?*

The doctors laughed as if I said something funny. Well, said the one that talked too loud, that's no surprise, is it?

The other one said, We're trying to keep that fever under control. You've been out of it here.

I said, I've been *remembering*. . .stuff from. . .before. This girl I met. Strange.

The doctors nodded knowingly at each other. The one who wanted to keep my fever under control was writing on my chart, and said, Malaria'll do that to you. Funny how we always think of women.

The other doctor grinned and said, Condition of war.

The two of them stood beside the bed, faces discolored in the sear of light, hallucinated, phantasmagorical. The one with my chart clapped it closed and said, We're coming right along here. We'll have you back in action in no time.

The one who talked too loud gripped my ankle through the bedsheet. You'll be fine, he said. Just give it a few more days.

2

I remembered my first action, Mamasan yelling huge consumptive sobs, lieutenant holding his arm screaming, Mamasan rocking. Lieutenant shouts he's bleeding. Still holding his pistol, waving it in the air. I begin dressing wounds. The widow's son: certain blindness. Both eyes riddled by shrapnel spray. Lieutenant shouting to stop. You asshole he yells, you never work on *them*. I look into the widow's face. She's staring into mine. Thump of chopper blades in the long sky. Pulled aboard by the door gunner. Then the hit. Then the dead.

3

At my grandfather's house my brother and I would climb into the cellar through the side trap after running hard in the alleys and train yards and along the river, creaking open the wood-slat door into a cool dark of mint and rotting apples. My brother told me a child had drowned in the river and was buried there, and I dreamed about the tiny skeleton going hard and white in packed earth in the silence under my grandfather's house. It was playing hide-and-seek through one August dusk that my brother hid in the rafters of the cellar, burlap hood over his head. When I finally pulled the side trap open it was full nightfall, a voice wavering from nowhere, muffled, in pain, *I'm buried in the ground you stand on.* I wanted to cry out, looking around to catch the glimmer of my brother's white T-shirt floating in a corner of the ceiling. The burlap hood made the T-shirt headless; the voice groaned. The ground under me leaned, my ankles oozed, cobalt sparks stung my eyes. My breath ached as sight failed and my brother was suddenly beside me, holding me up, his open farm boy voice in my ear, *Easy now, come on, it was only me,* his arms around my chest, and I woke in the hospital bed, soaked in the fever's glare, the sound of rain roaring at the windows.

4

Hot and wet and the night alive with insects, lowland bereavements, the taste of night on the tongue like an essence, and I lay in the middle of a vast heat, adrift in a cathedral of fever. Malaria dreams: candles flickering in a vestry as the ghosts filed past, gone but not forgotten, back to claim their visions of a time gone by, back for one more taste of the promises that failed them in life. Moving among them I presume I have died and the grainy shadows are the light of death itself. The best you can see in a dark place, a ragged edge of dreaming where blazes of glory might still ream the sodden air if you don't drown in the mud first. Or shoot yourself in the mouth out behind the latrine. Or simply go insane, running straight up paradise lane into the face of that mysterious enemy that lives in the air, riding in from nowhere, churning a wake in the dark scan of gravity's backslide, waiting for you, waiting for you.

5

It is that living, while it goes on, can seem like light itself, a perpetual slide of morning out of dawn's rare edge of perfect watery blue, light that leans and spills from a space in the sky between mountains and a roof of storm cloud, light escaping a doomed past to live again above our heads in passing glory. Standing in the hootch doorway, looking out at the morning rising before it begins to steam, and the girl who came to do the laundry said, "What your name?"

I turned, surprised to hear her speak. She was the typical Vietnamese child, looking ten years old but probably closer to fifteen. Not pretty, but a gentle face, a welcoming face, a wondrous smile coming easier than most. I told her my name. She offered her smile and said, "Captain?"

"No captain," I told her. "Just a soldier."

"My brother is soldier," the girl said. I nodded, afraid to ask what kind of soldier, where, with what loyalties, and I turned away, ashamed to be standing in her world, one more uninvited cowboy in town to kill her brother, and his brothers, and their brothers. Cowboys yelling like a drunken Saturday night, house of cards in free fall, breaking down and turned loose. I did not know how much the girl knew about these things. I was not going to ask.

Sleep ceased to be rest, was never an escape. Dreams careened, haunted, collided, and I was always forced to look: the double amputees, incinerated faces with lips burned off and teeth locked in satanic grins, bodies in decay and distended with gas, fingers and noses and ears rat-gnawed, the ones floating face down in paddies pulled out after days with tongues and eyeballs protruding from macerated skulls and their gunshot wounds looking so innocent, so simple. On the road out of a northern ville I saw a dog eating the body of a man. The man had been shot in the head, eviscerated, tossed aside. The dog pulled at a dirty loop of intestine, one paw braced against the opened belly. The passing scene on any ordinary day.

6

The medic who took care of me was talking, changing my sheets as I sat in a chair beside the bed.

"You know," he said, "for years they had no idea what the hell malaria was. You ever hear that story? Walter Reed in Panama, all that shit. Wasn't that where he was? Somewhere down there. Now you, you've got one hell of a case. You know you had a fever up to a hundred and six? Christ, you're lucky you didn't have convulsions. You've been talking, though. God, you've been telling some stories, know what I mean? Well, the fever'll do that. Swells your brain. No, really, I got a theory. It's like LSD or something, swells your brain, you don't know who the hell you are. . . . Hey, you rest easy now, docs'll be around in a while. They been real interested in you. I think they wanna write an article on you for one of the medical journals. Something about your fever being the highest they ever saw."

"I killed a man in his own house."

"You call those things houses? Shit, those ain't more than shacks."

"People live there. Spend their whole lives there. Raise their families there."

"That's their problem."

"His head was nothing but eyeballs and brains. I did what I thought I had to do. . . . I couldn't see a thing."

"Better safe than sorry."

"He was unarmed. He could've just said something. . . thrown himself on the ground, I don't know. . . ."

"Better not to take chances. I mean, shit, we're fighting a fucking war here."

7

The fever breaking ground, scattering, losing its grip and I was up at night in the hospital corridor shuffling toward a core of blue light in my patient's garb, standard military issue: SLIPPERS, HOSPITAL, ONE PAIR; ROBE, MAN'S TERRY CLOTH, HOSPITAL, ONE. In the heat of the disease I had seen a place where the past and the future were one, cleaved together like lovers rolling, turning, wide-eyed on a bed as flat as the sky. I didn't know if I was falling or levitating, and I wanted an escape to the safety of the present, clear of the terror of what had happened and could never change and sat like a leering man in a chair, gazing at me with a head full of regret and cynical wonder. From the hospital window the earth was a groaning body on its side, a face as empty of feeling as the heart of time itself, and I found myself preoccupied with the smell of the ocean in distant gulfs, the light on summer mornings along coastlines. Trade winds of the nervous system, the blind chemistry of need. Out there it was the dance of angels, the sweet dance of life itself where a man who was both too old and too young could reclaim a world as far ahead as he could see. If he could live long enough to get there.

SAIGON

1

Saigon, the elegant midday half-dark of the Continental Hotel's veranda, and we ordered drink after drink, all of them American-style: Mai Tai, Margarita, Manhattan, Black Russian.

"Have you ever seen a black Russian?" the American correspondent asked me.

"Oh, yes," the French journalist from *L'Express* answered, "there are quite a number in Moscow. I think many in Georgia."

"Georgia." The American grinned. "You can bet they're all over Georgia."

"I mean the province of Georgia in the Soviet Union," the Frenchman said, not smiling.

"I know what you mean."

There was a pause as the moment passed, and the Frenchman asked me how much time I had on R&R. I told him about the malaria, my reassignment to Saigon.

"You have been already in the war?" he asked.

"Yes," I said.

The American began to talk about the assignment his paper had him on. He was from a large midwestern daily. "I'm down in these pits," he said, "talking to these guys the MPs say are

VC shipped in for interrogation. And I mean these guys look like shit. They've been blackjacked and brassknuckled from here to Saturday night. I mean it looks like the MPs had been absolutely all over these poor fuckers. So I wire my paper, tell 'em I want a go-ahead to investigate the possible torture of American prisoners—"

The first subterranean shock wave interrupted him and he sat straight in his chair, voice collapsing to a dry whisper as the fireball ballooned out of the building across the street. The roof burst off in pieces, an aura of heat bowed the walls and flickered transparently, the windows vomited a palpable light. There was a second grunt under the street—the boiler—and I moved inside and behind the bar and lay down flat on the gleaming parquet. The Vietnamese bartender was already there, chin to hardwood. We looked at each other and waited.

Debris clatter on the veranda. A rising wind, or the sense of one; the sound of fire. A helicopter in the distance. The sirens started, one behind the other, unwinding the sky.

I stood up and from behind the bar I saw most of the drinkers crowded at the French doors, watching the blaze. I moved back to my table, trying to breathe evenly, ease the adrenaline in my blood, settle my stomach. My drink had over-turned and pooled over the table's veneer.

The American returned to the table shaking his head. "Son of a bitch," he said, "that scared the shit straight out of me." He picked up his drink and turned to look again at the burning building. "Must be a story behind it, though," he said seriously, sucking his teeth. He rehearsed a byline to himself: *Who's behind Saigon's urban terrorism?*

A dog wandered onto the veranda, a soiled waif, meandering under tables, whiffing cuffs. The bartender poured some beer into an ashtray and the dog lapped it eagerly. With its mange and bloody sores and starvation ribs the animal still seemed happy, and when I looked the dog caught my eye and walked wearily to my chair, lay down beside me sighing a vast resignation.

2

The call came across on a routine watch.

I was standing duty with Perelli, nervous Italian from Philadelphia who chain-smoked and kept busy cleaning the telephones with cotton balls soaked in alcohol. He was wiping a phone when it rang, startled him, rang again. He answered, listened, hung up frowning at me.

I was reading the office copy of *Playboy*. I did not look up.

"Sounds like a guy OD'd," Perelli said. "We better go see about it."

I asked Perelli if we really needed two guys for that kind of job.

"What do I know?" Perelli said. "Maybe they need fifty guys. So get off your ass."

I looked into the back office, told Master Sergeant Weldon we were going out on a call.

"Don't stay out too late, boys," Weldon said from behind closed eyes. "I'll worry about you."

Perelli edged the jeep from the garage and I got in on the passenger side. He drove out of the lot saying, "So anyway they don't know what the fuck. They open a goddam broom closet, he's in there lookin' dead."

"That's it?"

Perelli said, "You want more?"

We went in the front door of the barracks, Perelli carrying the aid bag while I pulled the stretcher. The corridor linoleum stroked back to the dim light of a rear exit, a high buffed shine. Nobody in sight. Silence.

"Christ," Perelli said. He shouted. No answer.

"You sure you got the right building?" I said.

"Of course I'm goddam sure," Perelli said.

He shouted again.

"Take it easy."

"I *am* taking it easy." Perelli said, opening the first door along the corridor. Paper towels, toilet paper, bars of soap.

Perelli pushed at the next door. A day room, beer and soda cans spread around the floor, overflowing ashtrays, *Sports Illustrated* and pornography slicks on a Naugahyde sofa. A radio was on, turned low, Saigon Armed Forces programming.

I opened the next door, not really expecting to see him folded on the floor of the closet with the brooms and mops, blue face and eyes half closed in lethal heroin nod, lower lip bloated and sagging.

His left arm was still tied off, violet stain at the crook of his elbow, needle on the floor beside his hand.

Perelli knelt to find a pulse. After a moment he looked up at me. "Nada," he said.

We stood together in the doorway. "Shit," Perelli said, whispering, "where is *anybody?*"

"Let's get him out of here."

"Christ," Perelli mumbled, "what is this, a fucking *murder?* I mean, where's the guy that called?"

"Probably eating dinner. Let's just get this guy over to the hospital, Perelli."

"Yeah, off-load him over there, forget this ever happened." Perelli pulled the body out of the broom closet feet first. The skull thumped against the floor.

"Now he's got a broken head too," I said.

"Shut the fuck up, will ya?" Perelli looked down at the corpse, and said, "Think we'll be in trouble for this? Shit, dead junkie, it's gotta be on our watch. Who is this asshole fucking up my dinner anyway?"

I looked at Perelli, my hands under the body's shoulders, and said, "He's my cousin from Milwaukee and you better give me a little help here."

Perelli grabbed the ankles. "You're a genuine smartass, you know that?"

We wrestled the weight onto the stretcher, belted the body down. In the corridor we could still hear the low murmur of the radio, the only sound beyond our labored breathing. The corpse's right arm kept falling as we wheeled toward the door. Finally we let it drag, down the steps, into the back of the jeep.

We delivered the body to the hospital emergency room loading dock. Two medics in white suits transferred the corpse from our stretcher to theirs, banged through swinging doors, and were gone. Perelli watched the doors, saying, "They'll probably try to blow him back up in there. Shit for brains in this man's army."

Back at our watch post Perelli slumped into a chair. "Jesus," he said. "Everybody dies here. Ain't one fuckin' thing, it's another. Everybody buyin' the farm. You notice that?"

I glanced at him, then away. "I noticed that," I said.

In his office Master Sergeant Weldon was reading the *Playboy*. "File a report," he said flatly from behind the centerfold.

Perelli got up and went into Weldon's office, sat down in front of the sergeant's desk, talking to the cover of the magazine. "You hear the latest, Sarge? Dead junkies in broom closets. No shit."

The cover of *Playboy* featured a blonde in front of a paper moon with her back to the camera, nude except for glistening black shoes, one spike-heeled foot hiked up to rest on the moon's bottom curve. She looked back over her shoulder, smiling at Perelli.

"I can't even eat my goddam dinner," Perelli said.

Weldon heaved the magazine onto his desk top, sighing. "Perelli," he said, "your fun has only just begun."

3

The river in Saigon was a drift of fruit peel and vegetable waste floating to the sea, children laughing and splashing in the shallows. The vendors began to line the banks at sunrise, cooking in the pink mornings until the smell of burning dung and camp smoke laced the scents of fish and water rat and distant ocean. A grandmother in a black *ao dai* set her stand up a few yards to the south of where I sat, spreading a ground cloth for the woven conical sun hats she sold. They were the hats worn by farmers everywhere in Asia, and she wore one herself. Her face was seamed, tired and beautiful. The Coca-Cola peddler squeezed his bell as he clanked his cart behind me, bottles ringing. I listened to the vendors' shouts grow into the day and watched the water move. A quartet of fighter jets blew over in formation, folding one by one toward the northwest. A Marine Corps helicopter labored past, rotors patting the air as the pilot braked for landing, and I could clearly see the streaked and expressionless faces of two soldiers crouching in the doorway of the aircraft, looking off toward open sky. The helicopter crossed and faded and under it, on the far shore, a group of schoolgirls rode bicycles, filmy white dresses adrift behind them like wings in the river wind and black waterfall hair swaying across their narrow backs, the high music of their voices traveling the haze and oily water as they rode, passing on south like a flock of mythical creatures in the fresh light.

4

I met Lwan where she worked, where I was alone drinking Asahi and vacantly watching the street when she sat down and said *You're lonely.* I was wary and said that I was not and when she invited me to her apartment I was hesitant. She courted my hesitancy elegantly, taking me up the fire escape past her cat into the one large room with the moon lying down on the ceiling, and we drank and talked, beginning to fall into the whole heat of taxi horns and bicycle bells and beggar chants ascending to a complete body, a musical politics invisible from a third-story window with the night engines of our arms and legs and the occasional helicopter grinding past at roof level so we waited until it passed to speak, beginning to fall into the space we made love in, falling and unwinding through to where I came back to her when I could and came back again and came back and always came back.

5

Dear Mary,

The ringing in my ears has finally stopped and it didn't end as I had hoped, a sudden freedom, but slowly, so I couldn't really know if it would ever leave me alone. Or it never ended and is ringing now as I write these words and will always be with me but I will simply be unable to hear it, my brain no longer able to recognize what it carries and cannot purge, the way one survives but is never again truly free. I remember talking to you about Jews who survived the camps and their madness and suicide and I can tell you it happens fast, it's not a dream and history never died. Time will pass and I will be standing on a street corner or standing in line somewhere, looking for all the world like anybody at all, another human being amidst the hundreds, one among the thousands, out on his daily rounds, living his life on any given day. Something will have happened in my life that festered, scarred, finally just sits, a photograph on the spine.

I remember the first time you cried with me, and the first time I saw you naked. And every time after the first times. Such memories are owned by the air. That's real safekeeping.

All my love.

6

"Where'd you do your time?" The supply sergeant was playing solitaire, snapping the cards into place without interest.

I paused in front of my new locker, dress shirt on my palm folded down to an eight-inch square. "Central Highlands," I told him. "Iron Triangle. Binh Duong Province. Around there. I'm on open travel orders."

The sergeant looked up from his game for a moment, then back to his cards. "You don't really seem like the Special Ops type," he said.

I jammed the shirt into a hole between socks and boots and sat down on my footlocker. "So who really is?" I asked.

The sergeant looked up. "Some," he said. "Some. You can be sure of that."

The sergeant was using the standard squad bay recreational table for his solitaire. I felt him look at me, at my back, and I turned around to see him softly pushing the cards into confusion. He stood and stretched, and lay down on the table face up, legs hanging off at the end. He got a cigarette lit and left it in his mouth, talking up through the smoke. "Livin' in the boonies with the dinks. Shit. I'd be fuckin' freaked out, too."

The sergeant was silent after that, exhaling like a beached whale. I sat on my footlocker, staring at the space of gray concrete between my bare feet.

7

Hawley yelling at me in the Blue Star Bar, "I owe you one, you son of a bitch! Let me buy!" Then, to the man holding him by the arm, "Fucker saved my life. No shit, man. I gotta buy him a drink."

He stumbled forward, collapsing over the stool beside me, elbows on the bar holding him up.

"Hey," I said. "Little wasted?"

"Wasted, hell. Just getting started."

"So what brings you to Saigon?"

"R and R, man, what you think?"

"R and R and you come to Saigon?"

He tried to wink but could not. "One of these goddam holes over here is just like all the rest. Know what I mean?"

I took a drink of beer.

"Hey, you son of a bitch," Hawley said, the words slurred, "I buy the next round. Bartender! Hey!" He looked at me, head wobbling. "Where the fuck's the bartender in this establishment?"

"She's coming."

A pretty Vietnamese girl in a black bikini stopped in front of us. She looked bored, and when Hawley grabbed at her breasts she pulled back, frowning; he began to giggle, laid his head on the bar, face down.

He giggled and said, "I love it."

I shook my head at the bar girl, and she moved away.

Hawley turned his head to one side so he could look at me. "Hey, man. No shit. You saved my ass. And I never gave you a proper thanks."

"Just the circumstances," I said. "Anyone would have done the same."

"Woo-wooo," Hawley crooned with his left cheek flush to the bar. "Modesty becomes you." He started to giggle again. I looked straight ahead into the mirror on the other side of the bar. The bar girl stood a few feet away, rearranging the top half of her bikini.

"You know something, man?" Hawley said.

"What's that?"

"I gotta take a piss." He raised his head slowly, looking around wide-eyed, a child waking in a strange place. "Gotta take a piss," he said, standing, one hand on the bar for support. He made his way to the table he'd left, falling into it, bottles and glasses spilling, rolling, shattering. Soldiers laughed and Hawley climbed onto the table, got to his knees, pointed at me. "Hey!" he shouted. "That man saved my life in the heat of combat!"

Hawley wobbled into a crouch and stood as if he were on a high wire, soldiers shouting him on, clapping, chanting as he pulled his zipper down, bellowing, "Here's a little tribute to the man that saved my worthless ass!" The bar manager was out from a back room, yelling in Vietnamese, pushing through the crowd.

Hawley had his penis in hand and let go, pissing a soft sparkle arc. The crowd made a space for the stream, laughing and applauding. The manager pushed in close enough to shove at Hawley's left leg; Hawley went down on his knees, pissing over his trousers, table rocking over on two legs with his weight, swayed midair and Hawley sprawled on the floor, on his back, laughter surrounding him and his prick hanging in the zipper's teeth.

The cocktail table banged over beside Hawley, rolled into a chair. I finished my beer, and waved to the bar girl to bring me another.

8

I picked up the taxi at the head of Tu Do Street, slipped in the backseat and gave my destination, and the driver moved off. Saigon at night: impassable sidewalks, mopeds squirting around and through traffic. Begging children ran to the taxi windows, pounding, yelling in, pushing scabby noses against the glass.

"Someday I blow this pop stand," the driver said suddenly. He turned to flash a grin, proud of his English.

I nodded. "May be a good idea," I said.

The car stopped in traffic and the driver looked at me in the rearview. "Really," he said. "I go to America. Get the hell out."

I did not say anything.

The driver held his right hand in the air, rubbing first finger and thumb together. "Money," he said. "Still drive cab, but live lot better. Maybe buy cab."

"Maybe," I said, watching the streets.

A horn behind us. The driver crept the car forward about twenty feet and turned back to look at me. "Got a brother Washington, D.C. You hear of D.C.?"

"I've heard of it," I told him.

"Got a brother there. He got a restaurant. Gonna work there."

"Good," I said. "Best of luck."

The driver's expression went suddenly grim. "That's what my brother write to me," he said. "Best of luck, he tell me."

I nodded at the windshield to let him know the traffic was moving. He nudged ahead, pushing against massed pedestrians, shouting out the window, turning across oncoming traffic into an alley. We moved into the dark slit. Naked and half-naked families crouched against the walls. A woman covered with open sores sat next to a trash can, staring straight ahead. She appeared to be dead.

"I get you fine girl," the driver told me.

"No, thanks. Got one already."

"Yeah?" He looked at me in the mirror. "Vietnamese?"

"Look out for the kids," I said.

He honked viciously at two children playing in a puddle in the middle of the alley. They ran to the wall and he looked into his mirror again. "Gotta do Vietnamese girl," he said. "Best pussy in-a world."

I repeated my destination. He took on his grim expression again.

We left the alley and turned right onto a broader boulevard, traveling briskly in lighter traffic. I rolled the window down, and the air that came into the cab was filled with the smells of fish and salt water and diesel fumes. The flag over the American embassy rippled on an easy breeze, lit dramatically from below by a spotlight hidden in the garden's foliage. Light gushed from a point in the ferns, humidity steaming over the garden, insects clouding into the beam. The driver slowed; at the next intersection the street was congested by a marketplace throng. I told him to stop. "I take you on, man," he said.

I told him again to stop.

"You gonna walk?"

I got out, walked around the cab to his window. He said the fare was twenty U.S. dollars. I gave him three. "Hey, man," he said, "not enough."

"Hey," I said. "Plenty."

He cursed me in Vietnamese.

9

Where I walked the streets were full, people and light and noise, shouting and garbled music and distant horns, cooking smells, the smell of urine, of cologned sweat. *Hey Yankee, you buy a watch?* and he was rolling a sleeve up to show the bright train of watches to his tattooed bicep. I shoved past into the fishmongers and noodle sellers and whores and boy soldiers, Chinese cowboys and begging children. A night like any other here, a dream disappearing in a sleeper's mind downrange of the moon, sleepwalkers' parade, a night drowning in its own breath. I looked up and saw a prostitute watching me from a balcony: we watched each other for a moment, then she smiled, waved. I waved and walked on, and at the Blue Star I turned into the tight room with too-loud American rock and roll, Jim Morrison singing "Light My Fire." An Americanized whore wooed a black boy in some kind of foreign naval uniform, shifting her hard hips against his leg, leaning forward so her little breasts fell into view in her halter. The black boy didn't know what to do.

I pushed past the crowd, through the back door, and up the stairway. Wicker stairs; bamboo lashed, lit by a single forty-watt bulb at the top. There was a boy sitting halfway up, eaten by shadow, maybe ten years old, and as I passed he said *Hey GI, you wanna acidy? Co-keen?*

I told him I didn't and moved on, stairs wheezing softly and giving with my weight as I went. At the top I knocked on the single door and a voice said, in English, to come in.

She sat alone at the small table with a dim lamp, dealing herself cards from a tarot deck. There was a black-lacquer bowl of rice and water chestnuts to one side, chopsticks laid neatly across the bowl. Every time I came it was the same: the small and dignified Vietnamese grandmother dealing fortunes, hundreds of different fortunes, amusing herself, passing the time.

She smiled at me. "Good see you, son," she said.

I put my right index finger on the queen of clubs. "Good fortune?" I asked.

She shrugged. "Good picture," she said.

I placed my order, took the moist fold of bills from my sock, and counted out on the table in front of her, over the cards. She bent to a cardboard box beside her chair and brought up the neatly packaged half pound of marijuana. *Cambodian,* she said in Vietnamese. Then, in English, she said, "Very fine now," and grinned. After a moment of grinning at me she gathered the money, counted it, slid it out of sight somewhere in her clothing.

"You good boy," she said. "Good Yankee."

"There is no such thing, Grandmother," I said, pushing the plastic bag into the lining of my jacket. She nodded, and her smile dimmed only slightly.

10

He was standing in the short hallway outside her door, face shining wet in the bulb's weak glow. *Hey, GI.* A silvery whisper. *You wanna work for Madame Lin? Make-a deliver?*

It was as if the boy sitting on the stair as I came up had grown to manhood and was still working the same side of the street. This older counterpart had a bright nylon shirt opened down his slick chest, wearing five or six silver chains around his neck. I looked down; his hands were empty.

"Madame Lin?" I shrugged, lifted my eyebrows, held up open palms, a picture of innocence.

He pushed his head toward the old woman's door; "Make-a deliver," he said again. "To American base. Business agent for Madame."

I dropped my hands, sighing, shaking my head. "You and Madame Lin stay away from the base," I told him. "They'll shoot you. Without a second thought."

He studied me.

"Really," I said.

He grinned abruptly: his teeth were filed, filling his smile like a yawning shark. I moved past him, hoping he was content to leave me alone. At the base of the stairwell a prostitute languished, bittersweet, smoking a cigarette. The smoke slid in front of her face. "Hey, GI," she said softly. "Take me home. I fuck you forever."

11

Perelli came into the squad bay and said a couple guys wanted to see me downstairs.

"A couple guys?"

"Yeah." Perelli shrugged. "Asked for you. Want to talk to you."

"You recognize them?"

"What the fuck is this, Twenty Questions? What do I know? They said they wanted to see you."

They were waiting in the watch room, a master sergeant with a civilian. The civilian looked a decade the sergeant's junior and wore a cheap summer suit under a blond crew cut. The master sergeant said my name when I came into the room.

I nodded, and he said, "Just a few questions." He slid two photographs out of a manila envelope, and I realized who my two visitors were. He handed me one of the pictures: the little grandmother identified to me as Madame Lin. She was smiling warmly, looking directly into the camera.

"Ever see that woman before?" The civilian asked.

I took the picture, looked briefly, handed it back. "Nope," I said. "Don't know her."

"Really?" The civilian stared flatly at me, clearly unbelieving.

"Where you guys from?" I asked.

The civilian stared as the master sergeant passed the second photo across: my face in blow-up, at the bar where Madame Lin conducted her business. I am laughing, listening to the man next to me. I remembered the night.

"How about this one?" the civilian said. "Guess you recall who that is."

I was feeling the first points of perspiration on my chest and belly. I looked at the sergeant and said, "Intelligence? Or military police?"

"I wonder if you could tell us where you are in this photograph," the sergeant said politely.

I looked at my wide smile. Hawley's right elbow could be seen cutting into the frame. "The Blue Star," I said. "You staking out the Star?" I handed the photo back, hoping I seemed casual, unaffected.

"That the first time you were there?" The civilian again.

"Been there maybe three or four times before that night. "

"That's all?"

"Yep."

"What for?"

"Excuse me?"

The civilian spoke in carefully measured tones, as if I were stupid. "Why do you patronize the Blue Star?"

I laughed. "Why do you think? What do you do in a bar?"

The civilian ignored my response. "You know who owns the place?"

"No idea."

"Ever been upstairs?"

"Didn't know there was an upstairs."

The civilian looked at me as if he were preparing to crush a distasteful insect; the master sergeant shuffled the prints back into the envelope. "Ray," the sergeant said quietly, "I think we've got what we came for."

The civilian continued to stare at me. "I don't think we're quite finished yet." He tried to speak without moving his lips.

I smiled sweetly. "Gentlemen? If that's all?" I moved back a pace.

The civilian turned to the master sergeant. "Let's take him in. Spend some time on this."

The sergeant looked at me clinically, examining the specimen, took a breath. "It wouldn't get us anywhere," he said after due consideration.

"Gentlemen," I said lightly, "best of luck on the investigation." I turned and stepped away, leaving them huddled together in the watchroom.

12

"So who was your guests?" The middle of the night in the watch room, Perelli talking in his underwear, T-shirt and white boxer shorts, thick hairy legs down to black socks and regulation spit-shined oxfords propped up on a desk.

"Don't sit around like that, Perelli. Somebody's liable to come in here."

"Cops, wasn't they? CID?"

"They didn't say exactly."

"Oh, shit. What you do?"

"Nothing at all, Perelli. They had the wrong man."

Perelli dropped his feet and opened one of the desk drawers, took out a candy bar and held it aloft. "My little stash. Midnight nourishment." He began to peel the wrapper. "So what you do?"

"I told you: it was a mistake."

"Bullshit, man. But it's OK, if you don't wanna tell your ole buddy Perelli." He took a bite. "You know," he said, chewing, "I was meaning to tell you. Scored me some maximum slope trim night before last. Prime cut."

"That so."

"Absolutely, man. And you know what? You'll love this. Know what?"

"What?"

"You'll love this. Broad's got her goddam bush dyed blond."

I looked at him, waiting.

"I shit you not." Perelli's teeth were brown from the chocolate. "Blond, man."

"So?"

"Well, shit, here's this cute little dink, what? Eighteen? Nineteen, maybe? Black hair, black eyes. . .you're checking her out now, moving the eyes down, nice little dink titties, and there it is. Goddam yellow pubic hair. Weirdest thing." Perelli took another bite of his candy bar and chewed with his mouth open. "So what do you think? Strange or what?"

I shrugged. "Just a touch. Entertainment."

Perelli gazed off as if he had heard something of philosophical import. After a moment he nodded slowly. "Yeah," he said. "Possibly so." He shoved the last of the candy into his mouth.

I said, "A little something to remember her by. Something to bring you back for next time."

He stood, stretched. "Well," he said, "I know where to find her."

"Be sure you pay her."

"I paid her, asshole. Fucking bleeding heart." Perelli scratched through the fly of his shorts and moved to the doorway of the watch room. "You think your buddies might be back to take you to jail?"

"I don't know," I said. "Nothing I can do about it anyway."

Perelli nodded. "Well, that's the truth." He balled the candy wrapper, threw toward the trash can, missed. "Anything I can do, just let me know."

"Just get out of here, Perelli. Take a walk."

Perelli shrugged, sliding off into the corridor in his white underwear and black shoes. I turned off the lights and sat alone at the watch desk in the dark, listening to traffic move on the street.

13

A fading field of vision, the world as it was meant to be that was finally nowhere to be found, lost of its own accord. A calamity of secrets in a mythical land where death was only a faint breathlessness in the quiet smoky shade of banyan trees. I would search my memory for Mary's face and the sound of her voice to find the glancing blow, the way truth can fail in the wake of time. I tried to dream about things that would persist. Things that might live on their own, impervious to change and random violence. I told myself there was something enduring and ageless about colors, and in the jungle I looked for them, counted them: magenta, scarlet, sienna. The blush of frangipani blossoms and heliotrope wheels of inch-high asters. Green, depths of green, iridescent and diffuse, the skin of canopied light all around us. *There are one thousand four hundred and thirty-six distinct shades of green in the typical rain forest,* an instructor told us at Jungle Warfare School. *White people can discern only twenty-eight of these shadings,* he added after a moment. I watched for them: emerald, sage, aquamarine, chartreuse, lime. Green as an apple, as the sea, as my helmet, as the filigree dragonflies that would land on the toes of my boots. Green as the river I was born beside.

When I thought of the jungle from Saigon the colors bled. Green had vanished. Elephant grass blurred and danced under the whip of helicopter blades. Yellow heat rose in a dream of empty air.

14

I went to see Lwan and found her gone. Apartment vacated. I tried to talk to the landlady but she did not—said she did not—speak English. She waved me off, irritated. Cursing. At the bar where Lwan worked her partner said she went back to the country, to see her family. Her father had been hurt in an American bombing raid. Where in the country? What village? Her partner did not know, shrugged, turned away.

Lwan had never said where in-country she was from. I had never asked. I walked the streets, realizing she was gone and I had no way of finding her, of even thanking her for the simple and hard-won things she had offered. Decency, comfort, innocent refuge. The street moved around me, alive with secrets, and I remembered a dream in Lwan's bed, an edge of memory riding in my chest, clairvoyant heart, each sound born to its resonance and Lwan's body's night curved to mine, openhanded as she waved me into a boat. I looked for a moment at the river fog before pulling in the rope, pushing off and out, drinking rain and oaring against the tide of my lungs, arms winging an open dark as I wheeled the light of the stream, levitating, two slow voices lit by star-filled water, sailing.

15

Dear Mary,

Was there a beginning to this story of the line? Standing on line, waiting in line. The line is a military invention, you know, a bureaucratic conspiracy designed to convince individuals they are anonymous and insignificant. Being anonymous and insignificant is fatiguing, and once you're tired enough you'll do anything. For anybody. One of the last days in the bush we came through a ville that had been wasted—razored and burned off. The bodies were piled to rot in the center of the village, rats and stench already there. At the edge of the clearing the sun was dropping in an elegant fan of muted rose that I might call lovely if I thought my feelings were intact. As though a hook can take you from behind and at the moment of impact you can't be sure if it's ecstasy or a pain so old and sure of your body it knows how to imitate ecstasy. And in this country there may be no difference.

All my love.

HOME

1

I was discharged from the United States Army in a hot room filled with other men being discharged, men exhausted by their faith in survival, their belief in the possibility of another day. A fading portrait of Richard Nixon hung between limp flags, behind a sergeant stamping forms in triplicate while I stood in front of his desk. The sergeant turned his chair to face a heavy gunmetal-gray typewriter on the desk leaf.

"Home address?" The sergeant's fingers poised over the keyboard.

I recited my parents' address, a memory of empty roads and uneasy tranquillity as I identified my home of record, the house I had grown up in and had given up as lost, as if I stared down a tunnel in a dream. As if my memories of a typical street in a typical town were only imagination, a legend of childhood deep in summers of rivers and old trees and trains, of distant voices.

Watching out the plane window I saw clouds coming apart in high pink winds. Against the sun some of the clouds looked the color of blood, and I was surprised at how calmly I thought of being wounded, lying in the mud with pantleg gaping and drooling, not sure if I had a leg, waiting for help. It was as if I were a blind animal in a canyon, alone on the landscape, following a silent river by the feel of water on my feet.

The plane's engines droned a steady line in my brain. Eventually I slept, dreaming briefly of a coffin. I was inside. I found I could stand up, wondering where the body was. The air was warm and fragrant, not what I expected, a lush and fluid darkness, inviting, receptive. I woke suddenly when an announcement scratched over the public address system. It was the middle of the night and I knew I would not sleep again. I patted breast pockets for cigarettes, felt the letter, took it out. The last letter I received in-country.

Dear Son,

Brenda was home for a visit last weekend. Isn't it amazing your little sister is a freshman at college? She's changed since you saw her last, grown up and pretty. She got three B's and two C's and your father said that was good enough for first semester. She says she wants to major in home economics. Your brother is still with that building firm but he and Marilyn are having their troubles we don't know if they'll stay together. Bad news—Buffy the neighbor's little calico cat you remember was killed last week. Mrs. Harmon said they came home and found her right there on the doorstep. She said the cat was just torn apart. We think it's a dog, that big shepherd from down the street I think. He was always a mean one. Well it's time for your father to come through the door and I've got supper on the stove so I better go. We all love you here and think of you often so take care of yourself as I know you will and come home safe. I pray for you every night.

Love, Mom.

2

We lost altitude over the water until the water was alive again and the aircraft met the runway flashing on a grunt and shiver of metal plates and tire squeak, hangars sliding the airfield's edges and California opening a flat sun-burnt haze forever, glinting over the hammered silver of the wings.

Inside the airport the PA system piped an orchestral version of "Norwegian Wood" and I walked along the rows of old women enclosed by shopping bags, mothers shouting at small children, soldiers drooping asleep in front of coin-operated televisions. A window the length of the concourse opened onto the runways as one of Braniff's pink and ochre jets tipped up and left earth, glittering in the sun. A woman with a suitcase on wheels bumped me, excused herself, and moved on and I blinked in the luminous corridor, following signs down a carpeted incline to the luggage carousels. When I recognized my duffel bag I pulled it off the conveyor, away from the crowd and to the end of the exit line. The business of any day at an airport all around me, the place and the people and the nature of the business well-lit and clean and comfortably efficient. It was a bright and alien world and I felt as if I had no idea where I might be.

"Do you have a claim check, sir? For the bag?" A uniformed woman at the gate of the baggage claim area.

I showed the stub.

"Thank you," she said, looking past me to the next in line. I stepped through the gate like a man getting out of prison, confused by the sudden wealth of choice and space. I shouldered the bag and walked in the same direction as everyone else. I walked a hundred yards and realized I did not know where I was going and sat down on a bench and watched the crowds traffic past.

I sat on the bench and told myself to relax. You're home. You're going home. I took a breath. *You're going to visit your grandfather, and then you're going home.* There was a public telephone next to the bench. I could call Mary, I thought. I could call the folks. I sat and looked at the phone. A woman moved in and picked up the receiver, dropped two coins, glanced at me absently as she dialed. She was beautiful in the strangely perfect manner of a magazine photograph. She began to talk but I could not hear the words. She looked at me again, this time smiling briefly, and tossed her chestnut hair like a mane, the hair catching light as it moved. I looked away.

After a few minutes she hung up and clicked past in high heels. I stood and picked up my duffel bag and walked, and when I came to an airport bar called The First Stop I went in and sat in a booth in the rear.

I drank tequila straight up with beer chasers, drank quickly at first, slowing as the alcohol waded into my blood. The lights in the bar grew auras; the bar girl's face seemed bigger than before when she came to ask if I wanted another round. I shook my head and she walked back to the bar. I watched her go and something in her walk reminded me of one of my sisters and I thought OK, I'll call home. At least I'll do that. I stood and had to reach for the table as the room dropped to one side in my head, slowly drifted upright again. I laughed, propping my duffel bag on the seat of the booth. I pointed unsteadily at it. "Don't go away," I said. "I'll be right back."

Two men in business suits in the next booth glanced up from their martinis, annoyed. I grinned at them, waved, and turned to make my way down the short hallway to the back of the bar, where a pay phone hung on the wall. I called my parents' number, collect.

My father answered, accepted the call. "Hey, old man," he said brightly. "You just get in?"

"Just got in," I said, slurring.

"You all right? Sound a little rough there."

"Well," I said, "matter of fact I've had a few drinks."

"Hey, celebrating. Saying goodbye to a few of your buddies?"

"That's it exactly, Dad."

"I remember. I've been through it. Feels good, getting out. No doubt about it."

"Yeah. "

"So you all healed up? Back on your feet?"

"Yeah. Good as new."

"Great. That's a relief. Really. Your mother's been worried sick. Ever since we got the news you'd been hurt."

"Good as new," I said again. I could see my father on the step stool in the kitchen, beside the counter, beige cardigan hanging open, unlaced tennis shoes.

There was a pause. I waited, my own breathing amplified on the wire. As if I were suddenly alone. The conversation was sobering me.

"So what's the itinerary," my father went on. "When do we see you?"

"Well," I said, "getting ready to head out. . . ."

"Where are you?"

"San Francisco."

"Hey, good town to get out in."

I looked down the hallway to the bar and into the screen of light in the corridor. "Yeah," I said. "Seems like it."

"So, anyway?"

"Thought I'd see Grandpa first. On the way and every-thing."

My father didn't speak for a moment. "Well, if that's what you want." He hesitated again. "Your mother'll be disappointed. I can tell you that."

"I'm OK," I said. "I'm fine."

"Well, sure, but we want to see you—"

"Just that Earl's place is right on the way, I can drop in and touch base with him. Just a couple days."

My father had turned away from the phone as I was speak-ing to say *He's home. He's in San Francisco.* There were remote voices, and my father came back on the line. "Terry just came in. You wanna say hello?"

"Dad, listen. . .just say hello for me, OK?"

"What, a few drinks in you, you can't say hello to your sis-ter? It's been three years!"

The men in business suits from the booth next to mine came into the hallway, walking straight at me. A wisp of fear started at the base of my spine. The men glared at me, squeezed past into the men's room. I took a breath.

3

I flew east on a military travel voucher. When the plane came down in St. Louis I went into the airport to eat breakfast at three o'clock in the afternoon. Sitting in front of the second cup of coffee I let the connecting flight time come and go. From where I sat I could look out at the runways, and I thought of traveling on to my grandfather's house but felt fine just where I was, between planes, my own purgatory in the middle of America. Somewhere out there and close by, I thought, was the Mississippi. Some of the same water had run past my grandfather's house, two hundred yards from my grandfather's back door, and I remembered my childhood revelation: the same water, the Ohio joins the Mississippi, together they go to the sea. I was, in the private ways of boyhood, in awe of the Ohio River. I read about the river in a geography textbook in Alma Norfleet's third-grade classroom, and later I stood beside the river itself, abandoned to its simple power. I was sure the river was mysterious, angelic, bound, I was certain, for the outskirts of heaven. My brother and I would fish from the banks, in days when you could eat what you drew from the river, before the shore was a congealed wick of paper cups and condoms and beer cans. My brother would squat and watch the end of his fishing line drift in the shallows and tell me stories about the river. Wild tales: mermaids and alligators, waterspouts, suck holes.

"You gonna be wanting anything else, honey?" The coffee shop waitress.

"No," I said. "This'll do it."

She slapped down an oily slip of paper. "There's your check, honey. You have a nice day."

She rumbled off with her tray and wipe rag. I took a last sip of coffee.

I found a connecting flight into a small city and took a bus from there, south, downriver. I told myself the bus would let me see the land again, the forests, glint of lakes nearly out of sight of the highway. But it was dark for most of the ride and I sat beside an old lady with a battered vanity case on her lap. She clutched the case as if it were a spar from a shipwreck, as if the bus were lost in open seas.

4

My grandfather pushed the screen door open with one crutch and looked down at me. After a moment he turned toward his rocker on the far side of the porch.

"Hell," he said, "you look all right."

Three years since I had seen him, and I did not remember the crutches. He had lost weight, seemed frail as he moved. I climbed the porch steps and leaned my bag against the door. My grandfather let the crutches fall across a glider at the rear of the porch and stood, unsteady, feet apart. As I approached he took me by the arms and pulled me close and embraced me.

We stood holding each other in the silent afternoon heat, and when he released me he said, softly, "I'm OK." He gripped the back of his rocker, getting around it stifflegged, sliding into the chair. "Just damned glad to see you."

"What happened?" I said. "What's wrong with your legs?"

My grandfather said, "Sit down, relax." He leaned forward to work a tobacco pouch out of his hip pocket. "I thought we'd lost you there," he said. "Couple times there toward the end. Least from what I heard." He raked a pinch of tobacco between thumb and forefinger, positioned it inside his left cheek, folded the pouch closed and tossed it onto an end table beside his chair.

It was the pouch I remembered, the one he had carried for what seemed all his life. Leather worn to a sleek gloss and his name on the flap, *Earl McFail,* embossed in gold. I sat to his left, the straightback cane chair that had always been my grandmother's. A chair for people who don't like to sit, she had said. The sweet odor of my grandfather's tobacco drifted against the smell of his roses.

"What happened to your legs?" I asked again.

He looked out, past the arbor to the empty street. "Hardening of the arteries." He spit tobacco juice into a coffee can. "Nothing to be done about it, I'm told," he said. "Not enough blood going to the muscles."

The street was cobblestone, never reclaimed as the western edge of the city declined after the Second World War. I had grown up as Earl McFail's house ran from beautiful old row house to tenement, the neighborhood in its final elegance a studied world of oaks and black maple and evening quiet, ivory doorknobs and brass knockers, stained glass and ivy in the perfumed dusk of Eisenhower's America. The street lost its owners to age and death, ringed finally by used car lots and pawnshops. My grandfather held grimly to his place.

Where his neighbors' homes had stood across the street a parking lot rode open and barren to the loading docks of the new federal building. Trash skittered on an occasional breeze.

"They were just starting to tear down those houses when I was here last," I said.

My grandfather nodded. "Didn't take long once they got into it." He turned and looked at me, then reached for his coffee can and spit into it again. The can back in place, he said, "So you came in on the bus?"

"Yeah."

"I thought you were flying."

"Flew into Wheeling, took a bus the rest of the way. Gave me time to think."

He turned back to the street. "Hell of a lot to think about, I imagine."

A paper cup in the parking lot began to roll in front of a column of air. "Well," I said, "yeah. That's safe to say."

Earl got rid of his spent tobacco, into the coffee can. "I'll tell you something," he said. "This war. I can't understand a damn thing about it. You know what I'm talking about?"

I nodded.

"You know what's been going on back here? You hear about all that?"

I looked at him.

"Demonstrations, marches, protests. You hear about that?"

"I heard about it."

Earl shook his head, resigned. "The whole damn country's scared. Confused." He massaged the thigh of his left leg, grimacing. "You see that issue of *Life?* The American dead. They had it set up like a yearbook. Faces and names, all lined up. You never saw that kind of thing in the Second World War, Korea."

The sun was suddenly gone, clouded over. The first heavy drops of advancing rain began to blot the dust in the street.

"Just kids," my grandfather said. "Naturally. No older than you."

"Starting to rain," I said.

He frowned at me, opening his mouth to speak, then thinking better of whatever he wanted to say. Raindrops slapped the canvas awning.

"Time for my rest," Earl said abruptly. "Hand me the crutches."

I reached the crutches across to him, helped him to his feet, moved across the porch to open the door.

"If I don't get a nap during the day," he said, "I'm worthless in the evening." He stepped toward me. "Wages of age, I suppose." He paused in the doorway. "I've got you in the upstairs front bedroom," he said without turning around. "Just like always."

"Thanks."

"Enjoy the rain."

"I will. See you in a while."

The rain was rising along the street and over the parking lot, misting. I sat in my grandmother's chair and smelled the air and watched the water move. I had loved to watch the rain when I was a boy, my grandmother with me as I stood in front of her at the banister, feeling faint spray stinging my face as the summer rains swept through the streets, across the roofs, against the windshields of cars, waves of cool air and the curtain of haze that held the rain inside it, a dream of pale light. Lightning caught and reached and was suddenly gone.

When the storms gathered over the river in late afternoons after whole days of slow heat I would wait for the water to break, to start with the first pelting drops and grow into the roar that came as the water opened and moved, that filled the air with the smell of cool roses and wisteria and wet wood, that razored the cobblestones, filled the gutters with froth.

Come back from there, my grandmother would say, tugging with a finger through one of my belt loops. You'll get soaked. You'll catch your death.

5

After the rain I walked out for beer, following the streets I knew so well, the years of coming back to my grandfather's house from the movies, from fishing, from the ruins of a fort on a wooded hill overlooking the river to the south of town. I was the boy lost in myself in riverside forest, establishing imaginary frontier camps with the muffled swallow of creek water riding light-filled over rocks. Earl had given me a tree identification manual for my seventh birthday, taught me to use it, and in time I knew by sight the trees that lined the streets and filled the city parks, learning their habits and stands, thinking I could hear their voices.

I bought the beer at my grandfather's regular bar; the bartender put eight cold bottles in a paper sack. We exchanged pleasantries. Yeah, just out of the service. No, my grandfather doesn't get out much anymore. Sure, he's doing all right, all things considered. I'll pass on the regards. Walking away from the bar as the sun was setting, I felt suddenly tired, as if I were as old as my grandfather, living alone with the hours. I looked forward to the beer's chance to ease me, a night's diversion, Earl's run of traveling salesman and farmer's daughter jokes. Welcome home, son, the bartender had said. Glad you made it back in one piece.

6

We ate TV dinners by the light of the television in my grandfather's living room. The Dodgers were leading the Braves in the third inning, 2-0. Earl took the Salisbury steak. I had the fried chicken.

"You eat many of these things?" I asked.

"Not many," Earl said. "You don't like it?"

"Just wondering."

"Don't eat it if you don't want it."

I looked at him; he studied the television screen. "Goddam TV," he said quietly. "It's changed baseball. Nobody knows what the game's about anymore."

"Baseball's different, now that it's on TV?" I looked at the screen, chewing.

"It's the intimacy that's gone. The subtlety. Baseball's a spectator sport, and I don't mean somebody watching a thousand miles away on a little TV set."

"You feel that way because you played the game."

"Maybe. But not entirely." Earl pointed his fork at me for emphasis. "You take football. It was made for television. You can see every damn thing that happens. There's only two directions to follow. There's a break in the play every few seconds. But baseball on TV. . .the essence is lost. You can't see the little things the players do, the signals. You can't really read distance. You never see the whole field at once."

"But you still watch it," I said.

Earl scraped the bottom of his aluminum tray. "Oh, that I do," he said. "Guess I just love the game too much."

"You want another beer?"

"I'm OK," Earl said. "Already had two."

"I got eight."

"You were thinking of a bigger party than I'm good for."

My grandfather had played ten years of major league baseball with the Dodgers, when they were still in Brooklyn. I had heard most of his stories. He was scouted out of the southern barnstormers—what Earl called farm-boy ball—and went to the Dodgers' centerfield in 1920. That first season he hit twenty-eight home runs and played in the World Series. Now the Dodgers were in Los Angeles and Earl McFail was seventy-one years old and he stood with his crutches in his living room. "That's it for me," he said.

"Only two more innings."

My grandfather crossed the living room saying, "Make sure the front door's locked before you go to bed."

"I will."

"And welcome home." He stopped and looked back. "You're a lucky son of a bitch, you know that? I'm glad you're here."

"Good night," I said.

7

In the morning I came into the living room in a pair of jeans and unlaced basketball shoes. No shirt, no socks.

My grandfather spoke from behind the morning newspaper. "You were going to sleep all day?"

I fell into the cushioned love seat opposite him. His feet were on an ottoman, ankles crossed. "Not all day," I said. "Guess I needed the rest."

He flipped one corner of the newspaper, looked across at me. "Left some breakfast for you. On the stove. You'll have to reheat the coffee."

"Thanks."

He folded the newspaper, dropped his left foot to the floor, tossed the newspaper onto the ottoman. He was dressed as he had dressed for business: charcoal vest, gray knit tie, pinstripe trousers, starched white sleeves rolled away from the veined hands. "Call home?"

"Tried to call Mary. No answer." I stepped to the tall windows that faced the porch and the street. A cement truck rumbled by, orange mixer turning a company logo into morning sun. HYDE CONSTRUCTION, round and round.

"And you were relieved."

I was surprised, looking back at Earl. "Yeah," I said quietly. "I was."

He dropped his right foot from the ottoman, leaned forward, elbows on knees. "Better call your folks. They'll be waiting to hear from you."

"I should get some of that breakfast. Before it's too cold." I moved to the doorway.

"Listen—"

I stopped, my back to him, thinking I knew what he would say. I waited and he did not speak and I turned to face him.

He said, "Is it hard coming back?" He looked straight into my eyes.

"Yes," I said. "It is." I averted my gaze.

He pushed up from his chair, reached his crutches where they leaned against the mantel, positioned them under his arms. "Must be mighty hard."

"Let's go in the kitchen," I said.

He nodded. "I'm right behind you."

Earl had left scrambled eggs and bacon and an English muffin face-down in a skillet.

"Put a little fire under that if you want," he said, following me into the kitchen.

"It's OK. I'll just heat the coffee." I struck a wooden kitchen match on the side of the matchbox he kept above the stove, lit a burner and put the coffeepot over the flame.

My grandfather settled into a chair at the table. I set myself a place across from him. "You want some coffee?"

"Sure. Only had about half a cup this morning."

I put a cup and saucer in front of him. Clean spoon on a folded napkin. The way he liked it. "Watching how much coffee you drink these days?"

"Oh, hell. Doc's got me cutting back on everything you can think of."

I slid eggs, bacon, and muffin onto the plate. The coffeepot was the same dented aluminum percolator my grandmother had used. I poured for my grandfather. "You take milk, don't you?"

"Jesus, boy, what self-respecting person would put milk in coffee?" He waved at the refrigerator. "There's some cream in there."

I found the cream in a miniature milk bottle with a fluted paper cap. Earl put some in his coffee, stirred. "Coffee was meant to be drunk with cream."

I grinned. My grandfather studied me. "You don't put on clothes when you come to the table anymore?"

I had a forkful of eggs in my mouth. I stopped chewing.

"Eats cold food and comes to the breakfast table naked. This what war does for a man?"

I swallowed the eggs. "I'll be right back," I said.

Earl shrugged, lifted his eyebrows. "Common decency." He sipped coffee.

I took the stairs at an easy run, the dark hall to my bedroom, and put on a fatigue jacket. The manila envelope of pictures was on the bed. I hesitated, picked up the envelope. *Is it hard coming back?*

In the kitchen I put the envelope on the table.

My grandfather looked at the olive green T-shirt I'd put on. "Not a hell of a great improvement. But better." He gestured with his chin at the envelope. "What's that?"

"Pictures."

"Vietnam? You took them?"

I nodded. "Vietnam."

He slipped the stack of photos out of the envelope and looked at the first one. After a moment he said, "Christ, are these bodies? Look like legs sticking out. There at the bottom. "

"We threw garbage bags over their heads. Only thing we had at the time."

He took the picture in his right hand, holding it at bifocal length and angle. "Three men," he said. "What were they doing there, right in the middle of your camp?"

"They came at us over the wire, yelling and screaming, shooting up the place."

My grandfather squinted. "Just three?"

"Just three. Strange."

He looked back at the picture. "Maybe," he said, "it was one of those last-ditch heroic gestures. You know, three men, don't have a snowball's chance in hell anyway, so they just go on in—"

"—and survive about thirty seconds."

He shrugged, putting the picture aside to look at the next one. "Well, who knows," he said. "Hard to say what moves people. Their choice might have made as much sense as anything right at that moment."

He studied the next picture, and looked up at me. "Why would you take a picture like this?" He turned the photo so I could see it.

I told him it was for proof.

"Proof?"

"We found him like that."

"Strung up by his feet in a tree? His head cut off?"

"We knew the guy. Found his head a few feet away. He was a Viet Cong cadre leader."

My grandfather watched my face. "You're telling me this was done by our people?"

"Maybe not Americans. But yeah, our side."

He shook his head. "What the hell's going on over there?"

I shrugged. "It's a war."

My grandfather poured coffee into his cup and mine. "Is that supposed to explain something?"

"Would you have believed me if I just told the story? Without the pictures?"

He pursed his lips, thinking. After a moment he said, "Probably not. War stories and fish stories, right?"

"Right."

He nudged the picture of the decapitated man. "And maybe," he said, "you should have just let me go on thinking that."

I took a drink of coffee as my grandfather picked up another photo. "Hey," he said. "Look at this."

I leaned to see the shot of a hooker I took in Da Nang. She had opened her shirt to the camera, grinning broadly.

"Yeah, I went to snap the picture, by the time I got the camera up she was showing me what she had."

"Which isn't much."

"Well," I said, "she's happy."

He began to study another picture. Through the antique four-paned windows I looked off to boxcars lined under the floodwall. The river rode the Ohio shore, and I remembered my mother standing at the sink during the months my father was gone on his second enlistment, in Korea. She stood pregnant with my youngest sister, blue-print housedress seamed over her grown belly, watching out the window as she washed dishes, across the backyard slot of rusting clothesline and fallow town garden, thin winter sun melting old snow out of the coal gondolas in the switching yard. She turned the dime-store plates and cups in and up and through the rinse, watching two open-end freights jerk slowly toward each other in the frame of the window. SOO LINE. ILLINOIS CENTRAL. CHESSIE. SNOW GOOSE. ERIE LACKAWANNA. CANADIAN CENTRAL. The freights rocked toward each other and she sat me on the drain board to watch.

On one afternoon we saw a derelict materialize out of the blank doorway of an orange boxcar, hesitate, his crushed Borsalino riffling in the slow air the freight made, and he jumped, sliding into a culvert and out of sight. The two trains coupled in a soft but terrible force we felt even that far away in the closed kitchen, rattling the big windows, and then the trains were still and my mother stopped moving her hands in the water and in the silence I heard her holding her breath.

"Now this one," my grandfather said quietly, nodding down at a photograph, "this one is just plain beautiful." He slid the picture toward me across the red-and-white tablecloth and sipped his coffee.

In the picture a huge Chinook helicopter came down in twilight mist. Everything in the frame was a ghosted shape except one face, an anonymous soldier looking out at the camera with eyes lit by sunset and angle and deep mystery, one open face watching from a home in chaos and distance.

My grandfather poured more cream into his coffee, stirred twice, and replaced his spoon across the saucer's lip. "Simply beautiful," he said. "You took that one?"

"Yeah. One of those moments."

"Damn fine moment."

I looked at the picture.

"Listen," my grandfather said. "Tell me something. You plan to show these pictures. . .to anyone else?"

I blinked. "Haven't really thought about it."

"Don't do it. Put these in a shoebox somewhere." I stacked the pictures, returning them to their envelope, and he kept his eyes on his coffee cup, pushing his spoon back and forth on the saucer. The spoon made a small empty sound against the high ceiling.

"They're too damned hard," he said. "Too. . .I don't know. Too true." He looked up at me. "I'm glad I saw them. But I don't know that anybody else would be." Shifting his gaze to the window he said, "Nobody's ready. You know what I'm saying?"

I watched his face a moment.

"I know," I said.

8

There was silence in the late morning light of the kitchen. When my grandfather finally spoke he said, "I'll be going to lunch with Riley Shedd here in a while. We're going up to the airport."

"Now you can eat at the airport?" I pulled the manila envelope of combat photographs closer.

"Oh, yeah. Some time now. Didn't you know that?" He half turned in his chair, leaned back, happy to talk about nothing in particular. "What is it? Couple years now, at least. Bill Clark opened a place up there."

"Close the cafeteria in town?"

"No. About the last place still working the downtown strip. He fills the place on a Sunday morning."

"I can imagine."

"We'll have to go up. Food's not bad."

"And a dining room that looks onto the runway."

"Matter of fact it does. The one runway." Earl grinned at me. "Watch the planes coming in from Pittsburgh, Huntington, Morgantown. All the big spots."

I grinned back.

The front doorbell buzzed and Earl said, "That'll be Riley. Let him in, will you?"

I walked out through the dark parlor my grandmother had maintained in museum condition: purple brocades of vintage furniture, shadows and gleam of polished oak and mahogany; an Edison Victrola in one corner.

I opened the front door to Riley Shedd, big man in a shopping center pastel suit, friend to my grandfather forever. They had grown up together along the river.

"Riley," I said. "You're out of uniform."

"Well, now." Riley Shedd smiled. "I'm a son of a bitch. The conquering hero returns."

We shook hands. I stepped aside to let him in, closed the door behind him. He looked me up and down.

"I'm out of uniform," he said, "but you're not." He nodded at my olive green shirt. "Kind of."

"The last little piece," I said.

"Might as well keep what you can use."

"Right."

"The old man around? Got a limousine waiting at the curb."

"He's in the kitchen." We stood in the sun-filtered gold and auburn shade of the foyer, Riley Shedd inches taller with hands in his pockets, jingling change. "You still a cop, Riley?"

"Yeah," he said, "still a cop. Pushing past retirement age here but, you know, the city fathers pressed me to stay on a bit longer and all that. I said what the hell. Don't have nothing else to do."

"Come on back," I said. "Earl's waiting for you." As we walked through the parlor Riley said, "Heard about you getting that medal. Made the papers here, had the whole citation printed. All the lives you saved. You should be mighty proud."

"Damn right!" my grandfather bellowed from the kitchen. "He's my damned grandson, right?"

Riley Shedd moved into the kitchen, stood in front of the stove. He glanced around, appraising, a policeman's habit. He put his hands back in his pockets.

"So, Earl," he said, "you didn't tell me the hero was back."

"Didn't know he was coming when I talked to you last." My grandfather pushed up from the table and asked for his crutches. I handed them from the sink. He positioned himself over them and stepped away from the table. "Riley's chief of police now. He mention that?"

"No," I said, looking at Riley. "Should be me congratulating you."

"Hell." Riley stood squarely as my grandfather moved past him. "Live long enough around here you'll be mayor."

"Who'd want to be?" Earl spoke from the parlor. "This damned town."

Riley glanced at me, lifting eyebrows and chin as he lifted his head, asking if he would be seeing me around. I told him to take care and he tapped my arm with his fist as he walked out of the kitchen.

In the foyer Riley held the crutches as my grandfather got into his suit coat. Earl said to me, "Ask a favor? That little patch of grass out front needs mowing." He settled a homburg on his head, adjusted the tilt.

"Hey," I said, "just like old times."

"Thanks," he said. "Mower's where I always keep it."

He took the crutches back from Riley.

"You two stay out of trouble," I called after them as they moved to the door.

"Too late for trouble," my grandfather said as he stepped through the doorway, into sunlight.

9

I sat in my grandmother's chair on the front porch. The morning was fresh, only a breath of the bright heat that would come. A bread van with a rosy-cheeked Shirley Temple painted on its side puttered past. I was thinking of weather in Vietnam. "Funny what comes to mind," I said.

"What comes to mind?" my grandfather asked.

"Fog."

"Fog?"

"I felt like I couldn't see anything. You're worried about every little thing anyway, and you're out there walking around and you can't see. Drove me crazy." Pigeons warbled in the eaves of the federal building across the street, fluttering out from ledges and back in, working their pigeon limps along the cornices. "Guy got hit by a jeep," I said. "Walking to the latrine in the fog. Driver just didn't see him. Walks to the john and gets hit."

Earl was looking at me. "Killed?"

"Yeah. Can you believe it? A world of hurt and you're walking out to take a leak and you get hit by a jeep."

"A world of hurt. That what you called Vietnam?"

I shrugged. "World of hurt, world of shit, Bonetown, the Zone."

"You had to kill people over there."

It was an announcement, a statement delivered without apparent emotion and it seemed sudden and brutal, although he had spoken quietly.

My grandfather waited, not looking at me.

I opened my mouth to deny it, to pass it off in some self-assured manner, and my hands began to quiver and I could not speak and I was in tears, helpless, gritting my teeth, crying. I sobbed and shook and closed my eyes and there was the heat of a fire too close to my face, blood fire. I backed into the tremor, clamped my jaw, opened my eyes and mouth, and tried again to speak.

I was breathless.

My grandfather pushed a handkerchief into my lap.

I put my face in my hands and waited. When I could breathe I wiped my eyes, blew my nose. "Sorry," I whispered.

"For what?" Earl said. "Don't be sorry. I should be sorry. I shouldn't have said anything. None of my damned business."

I blew my nose again. "It's just that. . .I mean, you're there in the middle of all this. . ."

". . .world of hurt?"

"Right. And you figure you won't make it out anyway, not a chance, and then you do and, you know, what happened? Where are you?"

"Why'd they give you the medal?"

"I carried a bunch of guys to a chopper."

"And?"

"We were under fire," I said. "Incoming. Heavy. We were bringing out a recon platoon, and I lost my partner so I got out of the chopper and carried in as many wounded guys as I could. Until I got some help. I was just doing my job, really. I carried them over to the chopper and shoved them in. They were. . .screaming."

My grandfather gazed out at the federal building's parking lot. "Remember when your father left for Korea?"

I remembered: the family—my grandparents, mother, brother, sister—seeing my father off at the train station. I rode my grandfather's shoulders, waving furiously. My sister was in a blue bonnet and black patent leather shoes and very white anklets and carried a dime-store Fourth of July flag. My mother's eyes were puffed from crying, but she smiled and waved. I didn't know where Korea was or why my father had to go there, but he looked extraordinary in his uniform, lieutenant's bars polished to high gloss, the toes of his black shoes buffed to a mirror shine. It was the kind of day that lives in a child's memory as perfect, with its still air and clean light and wash of virgin color.

The ride home from the depot had been uneasy and quiet. My mother began to cry again, softly, privately. My sister had looked up at me, confused.

"Terrible feeling," my grandfather said, reflective, gazing into an empty distance. "I didn't know if it was the last time I'd see him. And it was the second time he'd been in the army in less than ten years." He turned to me, a quiet smile. "Thank God I didn't have to see you off. I couldn't have done it again."

I sat in the fold of some final and complete desperation, thinking I could never explain what had happened or where I had gone or what had changed me. I was not sure that I knew or wanted to know. "It just seems nothing I can say. . ." I said, and faltered. "It's like wanting everything to disappear."

"Nothing's going to disappear," Earl said. "Except maybe you."

I looked at him.

"If you're not careful," he said.

10

"A peculiar thing, growing old," my grandfather said. "It's as if you—everything you are, your hopes and dreams, your wishes, desires, the way you feel about the world—it's all the same. The same as always. But the world has changed around you." Earl paused, looking at me. "You really want to hear this?" he asked gently. "I just realized how hard it might be for you to. . .grasp what I'm saying. The difference I'm talking about is not—I don't know, inventions and technology and all that, it's something. . ."

"Like you've lost your own time," I said.

Earl smiled. "That's good. That's pretty much what I'm getting at."

"It's how I feel. Ever since I got here. Everything is part of my boyhood. Other times. Things I loved that aren't mine anymore. As if I'm coming back here after twenty years."

Two clocks ticked on the mantel. "As if Vallie's been gone twenty years." I paused, and said, "We haven't talked about her since I got back."

"No," Earl said. "We haven't."

"I haven't been able to. . .find the right words."

"Not to worry. There are no right words."

"It's as if I'll walk into the kitchen and she'll be standing there at the stove, grinning at me."

Earl nodded, and for a moment his eyes were lost. "Well," he said finally, "she's gone for you too." He reached down beside his chair and lifted a half-finished bottle of whiskey, uncapped it, sat it on the floor between us.

"Might as well celebrate," he said, "seeing as how we're both old men now."

11

"So where to next?" My grandfather asked the question from the side of his bed, sitting in his underwear.

"Maybe Mexico," I said.

"Maybe Mexico," he repeated flatly. "Why the hell Mexico?"

I shrugged. "I want to travel. I've never been there."

He looked at me. "Think about things awhile, right?"

"That. And see new places."

"I would think," my grandfather said, "you'd have had a bellyful of exotic far-off places." He slapped his thigh. "And I could get you a job right here in town."

"I can't do that," I said.

"It's just what you need. Discipline, regularity. Besides, this is your home. You were born here. And I do still have some friends in town."

"I know. But it's not what I can do just now. I'd let you down."

Earl McFail was still in good condition. Defined biceps, full chest. He sat resting the heels of his hand on the mattress, looking down at his feet. "Maybe so," he said. "But what the hell's left at this point?"

I smiled, self-conscious, not wanting to justify myself. "I don't know," I said. "I really don't know."

"Well," Earl said, "no crime in that, I guess. Welcome to the goddam club."

"Listen: we'll have breakfast in the morning, like the old days. Fried potatoes. Sausage."

"Mexico," he said. "Christ. Stay out of trouble down there. And don't get the clap."

12

The second time I called Mary Meade's number there was trouble getting through. A succession of clicks and buzzes and the operator was on the line: "Did your party answer yet, sir?" Brooklyn accent.

"The number hasn't rung."

"I'm sorry. One moment, please."

Ringing. Between the rings a wavering wind: holding seashells to my ear when I was a boy.

Three rings.

"Hello?" Mary's mother. I knew her voice instantly.

"Hello." My dry rasp: I worked for the next word.

"Hello?"

I swallowed. "Mrs. Meade? Sorry—"

"My God, it's you. Where are you?"

"West Virginia. My grandfather's place."

"You're alive."

I laughed. "Seems like it," I said.

"Well, we haven't heard a thing from you for months. And I don't see your mom around much anymore. Is she all right?"

"Yeah," I said, trying to sound cheerful. "Sure. She's fine."

"I used to run into her all the time at the Safeway."

"Yeah."

"Well, I guess you're looking for Mary and she's not here." Her voice was crisp, simple and direct, as if the last time I had called was yesterday.

"Not around right now?" I spoke to take up more time on the line; I suddenly wanted very much to hang up.

"Listen. . ."

I waited. I could remember the set of Mrs. Meade's lips and chin when she talked on the telephone.

". . .so you're all right?"

"I'm OK. You know. Getting on."

"It's just that we've been hearing such terrible things about the war and all." Her voice went soft.

I wanted to maintain my positive tone. "I'm just glad to be through with it," I said.

"I'm sure," she said. "Well, I'll certainly tell Mary you called. I'm sure she'll be very happy to know you're back."

"Thanks."

"So when will we see you? Let me make dinner for you. "

"Well. . .I'm here at my grandfather's place. I'd like to spend a little more time with him. Not seeing him in so long. And my grandmother died not long ago. . . ."

"Oh, I'm so terribly sorry. You know, I think I met your grandmother at one of those cookouts your folks used to have. Her name was Vallie?"

"Yeah."

"She was a lovely woman. Cancer?"

"Car accident."

"Really? How strange, at her age."

There was silence. The distance between us roared. And then Mrs. Meade spoke again. "But anyone can go anytime in a car wreck, I suppose. I'm just so sorry."

"Thanks. Mrs. Meade? I better get going. . . ."

"Call us when you're back in town, hear?"

"I will."

"And I'll tell Mary you called."

"Thanks."

My hand was shaking as I hung up the telephone. I sat in my grandfather's bedside chair, looking down at the worn oriental carpet, tracing the patterns that whorled and connected in a roundabout of dead ends and threadbare intersections and stairways into open space.

13

Once upon a time I had been in love with Mary Meade. Loving her was one of the things that kept me alive in a place where staying alive was hard to do, loving her resonant image, the effigy of our touch. The truth that we were had its own home in some better time, a music played so often it could always be pulled back into hearing, but for the most part wandered all the back roads of need and desire. I wanted to tell Mary about things I had seen: the family living in a thrown-out refrigerator carton in the shadow of Chase Manhattan's Saigon branch, smudge-pot cooking fire, all of them crouching in front of the box as I passed, Mamasan, Papasan, five handsome children. And in the Caribbean, before I had ever seen Vietnam—iridescent hotels rising in background shimmer—a man, woman, and two children living in the gutted body of a lime-green Chevrolet Nova, damp diaper hung to dry over the steering wheel and the younger child, a girl, bathing her naked hairless doll in a road-side ditch. I wanted to talk about the roads cleared for the impoverished and the helpless and the dead, roads used for no other purpose, bone dancers turning in a white sun. I wanted to tell Mary everything I knew. That rain could keep us clean. That night was an asylum. That time was a lie, that the sky was on fire and in ruins, a long heat pouring over the edge of the world for miles.

When I first arrived in Vietnam I was assigned a holding barracks, waiting for my unit to move. I dreamed of Mary at the top of a stairway, looking down at me. I climbed the stairs, trying to reach her. I kept climbing and she was never closer and she looked sad, as if she pitied me. The more I climbed the more desperate I felt.

In those days before I left for the bush I sat up through the nights, avoiding my dreams, squatting in torpid heat outside the barracks door, smoking cigarettes and hissing smoke through my teeth, looking off across an endless airstrip waiting for the onslaught of in-country, ancient rage and the jungle's fatal light. I sat and waited, and the nights and the jungle were ghosts that would not speak as the past escaped like steam. When I looked out across that airstrip in predawn darkness, I saw nothing.

14

Waiting for sleep the last night in my grandfather's house I lay in the bed I slept in as a child, remembering the voluptuous spread of summer darkness as my brother and sisters and I ran into dusk, the flare of our cries running with the blink of fireflies, careen and cascade of breath, and the bright gasp of lightning behind clouds before thunder began in the distance of the sky and opened into us, a moving wave until the sound was alive inside the world, possessing it. Later, from our beds, we heard the rain begin and grow and rush over the countryside, an intense whisper, and the smell of water and wet earth was everywhere like a destiny, steaming in the moon's white voice.

Close heat and crush of jungle, walking through the cathedral light, one of a group of walking men in Bonetown, graveyard shift and random drift of memory and we are nine men. See us walking, and walking. See us from above, the shift of our bodies, boots alternating just ahead of our helmets, seen from above. We walk as if walking is the job itself, as if walking is all we are here for, walking with care, with respect for the possibility in the next moment.

On the seventh of June at two o'clock in the afternoon the point—first walker in this group of solemn walkers—is killed by an activated Claymore device. The second walker receives a fragment of the same device into the midsection, which enters via his intestine and exits across his spine, and now his walking days are over.

The rest of us continue to walk, although we have become confused about why, or where it is we must go, or do when we arrive, and we fear our destination more than any beast we might imagine, and it is the eighth of June, and the ninth, and the tenth, and we are walking, afraid to continue and afraid to stop.

ABOUT THE AUTHOR

Fatal Light, a finalist for the PEN/Hemingway Award, received the Special Citation of the Hemingway Foundation, the Vietnam Veterans of America's Excellence in the Arts Award, the Pratt Library of Baltimore's "Face to Face" Book Award, and went on to appear in over 20 editions in 11 languages. Richard Currey is also the author of two story collections and the novel *Lost Highway.* His work has been accorded numerous honors, including two National Endowment for the Arts Fellowships, in both fiction and poetry, a D. H. Lawrence Fellowship, and the Daugherty Award in the Humanities from the State of West Virginia. Currey served as a member of the writers panel for Operation Homecoming: Writing the Wartime Experience, a national initiative fostering the writing of veterans of Iraq and Afghanistan that led to both a critically acclaimed anthology and Oscar-nominated film. A Navy veteran who was a Marine Corps combat medic in the late 1960s, Currey now lives in Washington, D.C.

www.richardcurrey.com